Contents

JUBAN PE DARD BHARI DASTAN CHALI AYEE...... 159

Preface

The life and the way humans think, perceive and live are distinctly different in Indian metropolitans and the rural segment. This phenomenon is largely a fall out of economic conditions, literacy and social environment.

There is also a myriad of beliefs, myths and social practices that drive the rural society which is also the hotbed of corrupt bureaucracy that exploit the people and the system.

Here is a collection of short stories that I have penned, the themes arising out of real happenings in South Indian rural district of Andhra Pradesh. Of course there was also in the back of my mind the rampant rape incidents and resultant psychological catastrophes, coupled with Farmer suicides.

The incidents are in form of facts and fiction to give you, readers the pleasure of reading.

The book is a result of constant prodding and nudging of my wife Aruna, my two wonderful children to whom I dedicate this humble effort.

Temples of Desire and Other Stories

K.R. CHANDRAHAS

INDIA • SINGAPORE • MALAYSIA

Old No. 38, New No. 6
McNichols Road, Chetpet
Chennai - 600 031

First Published by Notion Press 2019
Copyright © K.R. Chandrahas 2019
All Rights Reserved.

ISBN 978-1-64650-575-3

Temples of Desire

Both were sitting on the parapet of the Tank bund munching on the salted groundnuts, peddled on the road by numerous vendors. Road itself was dotted by finely crafted statues in black marble depicting the images of the greats of the region.

Undisturbed, they sat in spite of the growing crowd of young couples walking lovingly holding hands and whispering with that known smile. The sun, now bright orange yellow, was submerging in the waters of Husain Sagar, the lake bang in the centre of the city of Hyderabad, creating a sheath of golden ripple across the entire expanse of the water body. Gold, Gold has been the most cherished metal from the advent of civilization

Vishwanath and his co-brother Raj Shekhar enjoyed watching Mackenna's Gold last night at the Ritz, after gulping down two masala dosas each and washing it down with cold lager beer. Raj Shekhar was much better off than his co-brother, with three fine eateries doing well in the posh localities of the cosmopolitan.

"I dwelled into many old manuscripts Raj" Vishwanath spoke breaking the silence,"but could not find authentic information on the formulation to try alchemy.* He was very well read and had mastered many subjects, specially religion and scriptures though he was a collage dropout. He needed money and big money to pay off some nagging debtors and for mounting expenses of four daughters and the son born last.

The third and the last daughter of Mrutyunjay Prasad was married to Sunil Kumar the Member of state assembly from Bhadrapur constituency, who was arriving the next day for a party meeting. Both Vishwanath and Raj had planned a big bash for the co-brother.

The MLA was never seen drinking at public places or even at his political battle field to keep up a clean image within political circle. his hunting ground was in the company of the co brothers. So it passed that evening after the hectic political maneuvering.

"CM has not agreed to release more funds for me to facilitate opening of Medical college and alternate market place for farmers, I am just about fed up with this paucity of funds with the party or the treasury" fumed the agitated politician.

"I am surprised that even after innumerable scams involving millions, money is not available?" interposed Raj, picking up a chicken drumstick to wash it down with vodka.

"Money has a tendency in our system to have an upward lateral movement Raj, very little percolates downwards to the constituency, you know that. Even for contesting every term, cash has to be found by us."

There was some truth in what the young MLA was suggesting' be it the schemes through the departments or routed via Non Governmental Organizations, the beneficiary ends up getting a fraction of the sanctioned amount. How much the direct cash channeled through the bank, as is being proposed, would be effective is anybody's guess as banks are now under the scanner for money laundering scams.

More drinks followed with heavily spiced, oil drenched food. No wonder then that the rotund MP with his distended waistline looked almost nine months pregnant.

"Your right is to work only and not to the fruit thereof. Do not consider yourself to be the cause of the fruit of action, nor let your attachment be to inaction."{stanza 47, chapter2, The Bhagavad Gita}, narrated Vishwanath, smiling at the MP.

"Your knowledge of scriptures and religious beliefs can be of immense use in my constituency", Sunil responded.

He represented an area of roughly 320 villages dotting around 5 towns, bordering two states, mostly comprising of poorly educated agrarian peasantry. The gazette had already declared the area as drought prone, the only work young youth could find was with few landlords or with sand smugglers of the area.

The bribe given to the border police per lorry, ensured free flow of material. Paucity of work and severe cash crunch had given rise to petty crimes. One particular community was deeply into robbery, thieving and minor crime.

The attendance at the Govt. run schools was far below the desired level. The veterinary as well as the Government Hospital were not only short staffed but were perpetually short of even common drugs. The persons who thrived in that area were the quacks and medicine man. The temples of Shanidev*, Ishwar*, Vishnu* and mosques abounded the area.

"Yes, our brother has hit the nail, Vishwa, we can build a place of worship around the divinity of a deity, or a saint. The challenge is to somehow build a myth around it to draw people in multitudes to offer their prayers and offerings." Said Raj, looking intently at both the co-brothers.

"Sairam, Sairam" exclaimed Vishwanath. The die was cast.

The great fakir* lived at Shirdi, Ahmednagar district, Maharashtra, an Indian state between 1838 and 1918. His Mahasamadhi* built by his devotees is visited by over twenty five thousand devotees each day. There are over two thousand major Sai temples built in India and abroad indicating the reverence and faith in the simple fakir who transcended the barriers of religion, inculcating in the minds and heart of his followers the concept of faith and compassion, the highest attribute to reach a state of oneness with the god.

Sai Baba lived an extremely simple and austere life, hypnotically attracting people and performing miracles, beyond mortal powers. "Sabka Malik Ek" the saying attributed to Baba was to restore belief in God.

The businessman in Raj Shekhar, the politician in Sunil Kumar and the performer in Vishwanath, the triumvirate, were helped by the local revenue officials in identifying the lands to be purchased at market value. The extent itself was much more than what would be needed for the shrine. No one was any wiser.

Any shrine once popular with pilgrims attracts kiosks and shops peddling items for worship, trinkets, pictures, garments, utensils and eateries as well as dormitories and lavatories. Raj Shekhar envisaged this and saw an opportunity for business as well as blocking other entrants by buying off large area of lands in the vicinity.

Much effort was made in spreading the word that Sai baba appeared in the dreams of the holy man Vishwanath and urged him to erect a shrine in his name for the good of the people of the area. An appropriate spot adjoining the busy high way was selected and the dalit owner made to part with the land for a consideration in cash and political coercion.

Was Sai Baba not revered by Hindus, Muslims, all creeds and casts equally? The other reluctant land owners were dealt with, case by case, as was deemed fit.

"It will help the cause of the temple, if you can try and get all the villagers to sell their lands, however big or small, surrounding the hallowed ground so that a certain sanctity can be maintained" Raj told Gopal Das, the sarpanch*, adding whisperingly though, that the headman could be made a shareholder in the three acres land on the east side of the Temple, where Raj proposed to erect a three star hotel for wealthier pilgrims.

The land belonged to Gopal's step brother. The incentive was meant to curb effectively any cross – current between siblings.

Very quickly rooms and toilets were constructed to accommodate the co-brothers and the staff. The old mud hut would suffice the purpose of a make shift kitchen cum dining. The tractor belonging to the burly man of the adjoining village would serve the need of leveling the vast expanse of land. All that was needed now was building up of the euphoria around Vishwanath.

Every deity, saint or a goddess has a special day in the week when extra or special offerings are made. It is Thursday for Sai Baba. Vishwanath locked himself up in the corner room, newly constructed for his prayers before sunrise, after the bath, much before the staff of six got up for the day.

Tej Bhahadur, the Nepali cook, Govind, the tractor driver, Jaya the maid, Girish the watchman, Prakash the general help and the driver, Raju, deputed by the MP were still in deep slumber. These persons would have a very critical role to play in time to come.

It was seven in the morning and the staff went about their work as assigned by Prakash, who was specially called for by Raj Shekhar to oversee the staff from one of his restaurants. He was well – versed in procurement of food items and accounting.

No one noticed the absence of Vishwanath who would generally be seen at that hour in the morning, feeding the stray dogs with the leftovers of the night. These animals have a very acute sense of smell and for some reason they were heard and seen whining and wagging their tails in front of the prayer room.

"Sir," shrieked Jaya, as Vishwanath came out of the prayer room half staggering with his generally well groomed hair all disheveled, "What is wrong with you?" then turning away ran towards RajShekhar's room," please hurry and see what is with Vishwanath Sir, he looks possessed "urged a visibly upset woman."

Everyone, present by now, were standing confused around the man who continued to look half crazed. Even the dogs were no better, wagging their tails furiously.

Vishwanath pointing the forefinger at the door of the prayer room beckoned the group in a soft voice, "go, see the miracle of Baba, who passed through me early this morning to spread the message of oneness with the god."

None had seen such magnificent pile of multi coloured cut roses in the region, nor had they ever set their eyes on the large raisins. The whole room was filled with thick incense smoke.

"Baba has left these for you as Prasad." Saying so Vishwanath as if in a trance re-entered the prayer room and handed each of them palm full of magnificent raisins, spread the roses in front of numerous pictures of Sai Baba and asked the maid to spread a mat under the shady tamarind tree.

None had seen anyone bring the roses or the raisins during the last twenty four hours. Has to be Baba's blessings, pondered Tej Bahadur the Nepali cook.

Nepal was the world's only Hindu Monarchy upto the year 2008. The populace of Nepal, almost all Hindus are staunch devotees of Lord Shiva. The Pashupathinath*, temple built around 400 A.D., with golden Nandi* standing guard at the western door is a big attraction for devotees and tourists alike, who also offer prayers at the feet of 5 meters long sleeping Lord Vishnu*in Jalasayana* at the Buddha Neelkantha village.

The earlier region of now integrated Nepal was fragmented by small territories and war lords, and is in this perpetually war torn Nepal,it comes as no surprise that in 2001 the last hereditary king Birendra along with his beautiful queen Aishwarya were shot dead by an intoxicated crown prince Dipendra and inspite of the peace treaty signed thereafter with the Communist party of Nepal, peace is far from secure and tension continues to run high in a society divided with a precarious economy.

No wonder India remains a favoured destination for the citizens of Nepal, looking for work. They too are looked upon as honest and dependable. Nepali Gurkha Regiment veterans who served in the British army during second world war were permitted to settle in England in 2009, for their integrity and steadfastness.

Most affected by the events of that morning was Tej Bahadur,

"I am blessed to be here, this very place is the abode of Sai Baba and Vishwanath sir, is his most cherished disciple." Saying so he to the amazement of all six and twenty humans laid himself in "Saashtaanga", the act of prostrating fully with arms, forehead, chest, stomach, knees and feet touching the ground, at the feet of Vishwanath.

Gently getting up from the mat, Vishwanath blessed his first apostle, looking meaningfully at Raj. The twenty labourers also partook of the prasadam* with mixed feelings.

Immense is the power of religion and faith as it turns into a mass euphoria if not channelized rationally, giving rise to all forms of religious corruption as is being witnessed of late.

The great communist leader called it the opium, deranging the human mind perhaps rightly so. The suppression of the masses and dictatorial tendencies of these leaders have had its devastating repercussions as history has taught us. That is a different story though.

The surrounding area, not too far away from the focal point, was abuzz with the happenings of that Thursday. The tea vendor, a good pal of driver Raju and Tej Bahadur, two furlongs away, at the crossroads, added many more customers while he talked about the miracle happening nearby.

Raj Shekhar had placed two large earthen pitchers full of drinking water by the road to let the people quench their thirst in the scorching heat as they passed by. Girish, while on watch, would mesmerize them with the narration of the recent events.

As a watchman, his routine was solitary and this opportunity to interact with young and old, especially in the evening, when batches of damsels, getting back from work, bare footed and thirsty, provided him with ample scope to get over his solitude.

Soon a stone trough was put up with water for the cows and sheep being driven home after grazing. Vishwanath was now often seen squatting in the shade of the tree, mostly in whites, deep in conversation with strangers who would drop by.

"Why should you have a separate prayer room, that too with all windows closed?" someone asked that morning, revealing a sliver of doubt in the manner he questioned Vishwanath.

"Friend, my body itself is the abode of Sai, when I think of him and pray and meditate, I see him only at the center of my forehead. That is where he resides, similarly every room is dedicated specifically for a purpose in the house. The prayer room allows sacred thoughts and divine vibrations to pervade the atmosphere and influence the mind in all its rejuvenated state, to perform "japa"* and "paaraayana"* answered Vishwanath solemnly. The doubt in the questioners mind was so settled. Vishwanath stole a glance towards a very appreciative Raj.

The second Thursday passed with almost identical happenings but for a doubled queue of people, who had come for glimpse of Vishwanath and the prasadam*.

Couple of days later a white ambassador car was added to the growing paraphernalia. Car was kept in good working condition by the driver for Raj Shekhar to drive on his own while he drove the Omni, mostly for purchases to the nearby town with the Sarpanch in tow.

Matters were gaining momentum and so was Gopal Das who had by now graduated to a sort of manager, purchasing provisions etc. for the everyday needs of the set up growing constantly. A small part of the purchases diverting to the dwellings of his keep in the town.

"Beware of the sarathi*", the saying goes thus in old scripts "as he sees all". Raju's share of the spoils was taken care of by Gopal Das. The cleaning woman often wondered at the recent spotting of Red Horse malt whisky bottles in the ditch facing the hallowed grounds, across the high way.

Very few of the visitors were allowed into the prayer room. Vishwanath made arrangement for a potted Tulasi* plant to be kept near the door of the Sanctum Sanctorum.

The area was well kept by plastering the ground with cow dung and decorating the pot with vermillion and turmeric.

Devotees started bringing flowers and coconuts as offering.

"Why Tulasi plant sir?" enquired the line man' who would be there at the evening conclave without fail every day. His seven year old son was hopelessly suffering with paralysis of the lower limbs.

"Tula naanaasti athaiva tulasi*, it is incomparable and sacred of all the plants. Lord Krishna has given it a special status, as well as power to heal many ailments" explained

Vishwanath, so satiating the quarry of a devout and simple muslim. Ahmed next day bought home a Tulasi plant and placed it in front with all reverence. "Sabka Malik Ek".

Gradually the visitors swelled in numbers, so did the coconuts. Every Thursday, now a cook would specially come to make coconut burfi.* Sugar and coconut heated and made into squares with a dash of cardamom. This now was the official prasadam.

Of course Gopal Das always managed to take kilo or two for his concubine. Expenses were mounting, Raj Shekhar started draining his resources too from the business for he was sure of the enterprise the three had embarked upon.

Monsoons had passed and moderate chill could be felt now since the advent of the saga. The events of Thursday was drawing serpentine queue of devotees as well as skeptics. It is at this stage that Raj Shekhar drove away to the big city in his Ambassador alone, leaving enough resources with Prakash to ensure smooth functioning of the estate.

It is a common sight in India to witness scores of people in groups, wearing normal clothes or all of them dressed alike in bright yellow, red or black proceeding barefooted to far away temples and shrines as part of a vow, facing all the hardship associated with the ordeal.

Tej Bahadur would watch similar groups walk by slowly vanishing in the horizon and a sense of deep devotion would swell up in his whole being. Great was his expectation to catch a glimpse of Sai baba, after all has not Vishwanath Sir mentioned that Baba can appear in any form at the temple site?.

Gradually Ahmed became the most frequent of the believers. He would often bring saplings of Marigold, Jasmin, Kanakambaram, a gift from his friend, the guard, from the nursery of forest department and plant them in a neat row, on one side of the sanctum sanctorum.

"Bread feeds the body indeed, but flower feeds also the soul" words attributed to Prophet Mohammed, would often be the explanation of the devout Muslim.

Unkempt and bearded mendicants, resembling the great Fakir would stop by giving the estate a forlorn look thus prompting the Nepali to rupture in ecstasy and follow the lone passerby who would generally accept the food and alms in silence and walk away uttering blessing.

Soon the tea vendor at the crossroad was heard speaking of the visits of Sai Baba. Such is the power or effect of religion and faith, across the human race that it defies logic and subdues even the acute pain of flesh burning as is being witnessed time and again by Buddhist monks opting for self-immolation on one side and Jehadis, using themselves as human bomb to eradicate or inflict pain on fellow humans who they perceive as non believers or Kafirs*.

Raj Shekhar returned from his undisclosed destination, two men in tow.

"Make arrangement for their stay Prakash, they are master marble cutters from city, I have also arranged for blocks of marble and the circular cutting machine".

Soon a shed was erected at the temple site to accommodate the equipment. The foundation and the platform had to be erected. It was already eighth month, and the expectation of the populace was constantly increasing. Vishwanath sensed a feeling of skepticism in the air.

Large conclave of devotees had gathered that Thursday. Word had spread that something unusual might happen being Sai Baba's birthday as given in the documented chronology. People had flocked from far and wide, walking, on motorcycles and cars.

Few limos could be seen too dropping dented and painted women, in deep devotion along with pot-bellied men. Mostly in whites, who represented particular profession. Politics, the qualification to practice that, is to look for trouble, find it everywhere, diagnose it incorrectly and treat it with wrong remedies. Religion and politics as the detached crusader, the greatest of the man among few in last many centuries said,

"Those who say that religion has nothing to do with politics. Do not know what politics is." Mohan Das Karamchand Gandhi was never far from the truth then and now.

Great was the expectation and far greater was the spectacle when a completely disheveled Vishwanath came out of the prayer room grabbing hold of Ahmed, standing guard at the door, spoke to the District Collector in a very feeble voice,

"Friend, Baba has indeed blessed all of us, please come in."

That day to the amazement of regulars, as well as first timers, seven ivory white statues of Sai were seen, surrounded with the usual roses and raisins. Bending twice with folded hands, Vishwanath lifted two of the statues and put them in the open palms of the Collector and Ahmed. Amid chants of Ram Sai, ShyamSai reverberating, the five remaining statues were gifted to the wives of the politicians gathered that day.

There was a sea change in the atmosphere at the site. Mild winter chill had set in, loud whirring sound of the disk cutting through the marble blocks could be heard throughout the day and sometimes till late in the night. The Electricity Board had granted the permission for current to be available 24/7 at the temple site.

The number of devotees had swelled many folds. All the land documentations were completed in record time. The sole registered owner being Raj Shekhar, the managing trustee. The patriarchal, eighty two years, Ramakanth Goenka, Chairman of City Link Bus Service had placed two vehicles to ferry people to and fro from bus stands every Thursday.

Large cauldrons full of rice. Curry and pickle would be sent by Kamadhenu Milk Products Ltd from their factory premises near by for the devotees. Permitted by Raj Shekhar, paper plates were being sold by Gopal's son. The tea vendor was roped in to sell tender coconut and bottled water for the devotees who could afford it.

The offerings increased too, specially flowers and coconuts with the fibre covering removed, retaining the tuft on the top. The temples and the shrines all over the country receive offerings of the nut as it symbolizes selfless service. The fruit, leaves, coir and the trunk is useful in making soap, oil, mats, dishes and ropes. The tree takes in the salty water from the soil and converts it into sweet water having medicinal value.

No wonder then that people revere it as the Shri Phala.*

"How are you today?" enquired Vishwanath seeing Ahmed along with three others, walk in through the gates.

"Haza Min Fazali Rabbi", he replied smiling in Arabic. I am the way, Lord has willed it for me, meant Ahmed. The MP, Sunil Kumar was much amused and shook hands with the visitors. Every day if time permitted, Ahmed would go for his namaz and after the prayers would interact with fellow namazis about the socio-political scenario, Holy book and the happenings at the upcoming Sai temple.

Gradually few more Muslims started gathering at the evening conclave out of curiosity and faith on the saint. Sufi's and saints are much revered in Islamic way of life like the Haji Ali of Mumbai, Saint of Ajmer Sharif, Salim Chisti near Agra or the great Mohammed Aullia of Shahajanabad near Delhi.

This intermingling of faith suited the MP, whose visits to the site had become more frequent now. Elections were sixteen months away.

This part of the country side had two major parties and a third one had emerged causing polarization of the vote bank, specially the minority was apprehensive of its labeled rightist alignment. The Election commission had allotted it the symbol of a large flower resembling a lotus.

Sunil Kumar's political outfit and the new entrants had decided to cooperate in formation of the government in case the need arose, and a lot of effort was called for in diluting misrepresentations and false propaganda. The major existing players had bullock cart and plough as their symbols for better affinity with the populace, mostly agrarian.

"But why this flowery symbol, in an area where we do not even see such species?," enquired Mehboob of the MP, knowing well the strategy and need for alignment of both the parties. Sunil Kumar was at his wits end not being a trained orator.

"I cannot say why the party has taken to that symbol but the lotus blooms at the sunrise and folds in its petals at night fall. Knowledge is like light, expanding our mind, and darkness symbolizes ignorance when we should also close our mind to avert the effects of it."

"Lotus thrives in muddy waters but remains untainted despite its surroundings, reminding us that we should too remain unaffected and remain ever joyous in this world of sorrow and change, lest we become a mere tear drop on the cheek of time. Lotus does not allow a single drop of water to wet it, though it is almost submerged in water." explained Vishwanath carefully avoiding any reference to scriptures, satisfying Mehboob and bringing relief to a gratified politician.

How right I was to get them to undertake this endeavour thought Sunil Kumar. Inspite of the plans the three had put in action, one matter continued to disturb him, though a wily politician good at managing events and people, he was unable to contain the demand of Vishwanath to keep him supplied with cough syrup bottles in large quantities.

The M.P. was unaware of the real purpose of consuming couple of bottles of the soothing syrup and whenever he enquired from Raj Shekhar, he would receive the same reply with a grin.

"Oh, let him be, it is good for his throat, chest and general well-being".

Vishwanath needed his sedative often as what else but Diphenhydramine, an anti-allergic compound present in the sedatives, available off the counter would suit? Its anti-cholinergic effect would cause some delirium and light headedness enough to keep Vishwanath happy and camouflaged too. Raj was well aware of the epicurean tendencies, apart from an eye for the fairer sex, of his co-brother.

The process went on till the foundation and the platform of the temple was in place. Many a devotees received statues of Sai with gratitude. All the offers of cash donations were put on hold. Rajshekhar knew that acceptance of donation in cash not only will dilute people's faith but also would result in interference.

It is around this time that the political equation took an unprecedented turn. Many from the ruling party crossed over to the new outfit with the flower symbol. It is said much money changed hands in the horse trading that went on. Sunil Kumar, along with his entourage of three MLAs, jumped the wagon too, hoping to be in a commanding position to dictate terms when the alliance would be in place while forming the government.

Campaigning was loud and hectic. The election commission had not found its teeth then. Politicians of all hues came to Vishwanath to seek Baba's intervention. Raj too, very actively campaigned.

However the voters decided that the alliance was an unholy one.

Not far away from the town, the Government had acquired some land to set up Agriculture Producers Marketing infrastructure and cold storage facility for fruits. Some multinational companies were also actively lobbying with the state Chief Minister and others to provide them with enhanced and better power supply to set up manufacturing plants.

The place was well connected to sea and air ports apart from a moderate climate. The rate paid was much higher now than what RajShekhar had given for the lands. The water was insufficient, though if bored deeper, uninterrupted supply of it could be ensured and the mildly cold climate was suitable for vegetable crops like cabbage, capsicum, carrot, baby corn farming*, involving small and large farmers, to procure gherkins and Baby corn etc.

The corn is generally used to make savoury pickled with cucumber in vinegar or brine, four to eight centimeter in length, often flavoured with herbs like dill. It is used as an accompaniment in sandwiches in Europe mostly. Potential of export has attracted many joint ventures. The Baby corn too is largely exported to far east, The stalk itself is soft and sweetish and makes a great fodder for milking cows.

It is in this background that lot of movement was observed of people walking around the vast lands opposite the temple site, holding maps and some instruments.

They were Hydro Geologists from city. Later in the week even more persons were observed holding odd items and walking around. They were water diviners. Known as dowsing, is an attempt to locate underground water sources using bent rods, pendulums, forked stick, while walking in a given area. If this works or not is anyone's guess, and general belief is that the diviner guesses the source of water finding some old buried pipes, contour of the land and vegetation etc.

Soon the word was out. The German retail giant was setting shop in the country after the Centre had permitted forty nine percent stake holding by foreign multinational. The lands were being surveyed for feasibility and price fixation for the Foreign Direct Investor [FDI] to grow exotics and for cold storage facility.

The land rate is bound to jump many folds thought Raj Shekhar. His long absence from the city had caused the business to slow down to a considerable extent and the expenses at the temple site also had far over reached the original estimates. MLA, losing the election had dashed all hopes of political and monetary favours.

He barely slept that night, tossing around in the bed, thoughts racing about in his mind.

He had fairly worked out his moves by morning, for commonly, "where so ever God buildeth a church, the devil will build a chapel just by".

Jaya, the maid's indulgence, is what he desired the most now. Raj till now had not paid any heed to the repeated requests of the woman for an advance before the monsoon set in, to mend the thatched roof of her hut in the village where her ailing mother and young daughter lived. Raj had also sensed the devotion and admiration she had for Vishwanath. He let a couple of days pass by before he called the woman to his make – shift office.

"Rains may start in some five to six weeks now Jaya, I was thinking of asking Govind to get three to four acres ready with the tractor to sow in different vegetable seeds or saplings. These days we have many guests to feed during the day" said RajShekhar, testing the waters and prompting the maid to reopen the subject of the repairs, weighing on her mind heavily.

"Yes Sir, it would be good to plant six to seven varieties of vegetables along with potato," replied Jaya, hoping that the talks would lead to her requirement of cash needed so desperately, just when the sarpanch Gopal Das entered the office, much to Jaya's disappointment at the abrupt and untimely interference.

"Come Gopal and take a seat, I was just talking to Jaya of her requirement for an advance to repair the roof of her thatched hut. What do you feel this would cost?"enquired RajShekhar with a twinkle in his eyes.

It took but a few cross questions from the Sarpanch and the matter was concluded with the amount being fixed in a way that the woman would have the repairs done and still have some cash left for her personal needs. Gopal was asked to fix the artisans, as well as, see to the broader objective in RajShekhar's mind.

The financial transactions in this part of the country side was done by the borrower signing a promissory note at an usual interest rate of two percent per month, executed in presence of two or more witnesses. Honouring the agreement in almost all the cases would result in long delays causing the individual or the peasant to lose the lands or re-borrowing from other sources causing the vicious circle of interest burden to continue to his progeny.

Media reports of suicide due to debt burden are a recurring news item in papers. Jaya's case was different as she realized later. All RajShekhar desired now was to create a fusion by squaring up the circle, bringing together a woman's curve and a man's angle. Gopal used his position as the elected chief of a cluster of hamlets, to get the artisans to finish up the repairs and pocketed the usual percentage while settling the accounts.

Rajshekhar's eldest daughter Sangeeta had moved in from the city to the temple site for a couple of weeks after her final graduation exams and occupied the hall near the prayer room adjoining the bed rooms of the co-brothers.

"It is needed that you shift to the site now" said RajShekhar addressing Jaya.

"Someone needs to be with Sangeeta at nights, and you are the only one I can entrust this function" he continued staring vaguely at the setting sun, avoiding direct eye contact with the woman.

"That way you may be able to keep an eye at the shade net, after all it contains thousands of saplings, an easy target for the stealing rouges of your own village. Take off to your village in the afternoon, it is only a mile away and be back before sunset".

The construction work of the temple was put on hold due to rains but the evening congregation continued as usual and was feverishly assuming an earnest belief of the reality and beneficence of a supernatural power, surrounding the great saint undisputedly by both Muslims and Hindus alike.

Sai Baba of Shirdi anyway is said to have lived in a mosque but cremated by Hindu devotees.

Night falls early in the country side and generally the day is wound up by nine to cope with the grueling field work the next day. Sangeeta too fell in the routine.

"Why don't you go and massage Vishwanath Sir's legs after Sangeeta sleeps, anyway you can pretend to go to staff quarters if she asks" prompted RajShekhar,

"He now has swollen limbs due to constantly sitting in the pooja room and mind you do not mention that I suggested this," warned RajShekhar as he continued staring deep into the maids eyes to read her thoughts.

Jaya needed no more prompting for she was much in awe of the lascivious holy man. Although the repetitive occurrence of the act thereafter had a devastating effect on the mind-set of the people and happenings as will come out later.

The hardening in between the thighs of Vishwanath when Jaya tenderly massaged his limbs was enough to bring about coitus under the benevolent eyes of the Gods themselves.

This did not take long to produce the desired effect that Raj wanted. The expectations from holy men in all faiths, is similar on the subject of morality and self-conduct. Asaram, the self styled God man of Gujarat will vouch for it, as he cools his heels in the prison for molesting woman.

What stands out glaringly is the immediate subjugation of woman to the dark depths of hell. There were whispers and discussions everywhere and persons most disturbed and probed were Ahmed and TejBahadur. The Nepali would shrug his shoulder, spoke inaudibly something and found solace among the pots and pans, a beedi dangling from his charred lips.

Ahmed was vociferous and would quote from a Persian poet, "In the beginning, Allah took a rose, a lily, a dove, a serpent, little honey, a dead sea apple and a handful of clay, when he looked at the amalgam, it was a woman." He would say scornfully, spitting and gesturing as if throwing a stone at Jaya emulating Taliban's recent penalizing of women, supposedly for the acts of adultery.

Far reduced was now the gathering in the evenings and it took all but some seven weeks before the devotees coming from far away dwindled in numbers causing Seth Ramakanth to halt the bus service. Sunil Kumar, the MLA had already distanced himself fearing a backlash of public opinion. It is at this stage that the matter went as far as the city to the wife of Vishwanath.

All hell broke loose as Sangeeta back from the site narrated the happenings to the distraught lady.

Vishwanath himself now a very beleaguered man could not bring himself to face the family or the thinned down conglomeration of faithfuls, but continued the rituals as well as distribution of the white marble statues now very occasionally.

Ahmed had altogether broken himself away and, except Seth Ramakanth Goenka, no one of any importance would be seen at the site. Humans have the audacity to wonder as to why the Almighty has meted out punishment thus and that evening Vishwanath interposed the same to the Seth, himself a very learned and well-read individual, who pensively recited in Sanskrit,

"UddhareDaatmaanathman,
NathmaanamVasadayeth,
AthmivaRaathmano,
Bandhuraathmiva, Ripuraathman."

"One should lift oneself by one's own efforts and should not degrade oneself, for one's own self is ones friend, and one's own self is ones enemy"….{Chapter 6, Stanza 5 The Bhagavad Gita}

Saying so the Seth departed shaking his balding head never to return again.

The atmosphere at the site was depressing too. Once a very congenial and friendly relationship between the staff had turned visibly strained now. Faith having diminished had given way to petty squabbles and disenchantment. Suspicion was in the air. The Nepali was seen wandering about at night in a daze, deep in thoughts near the dwellings and the construction site.

During one such night, late into the witching hour a slight drizzle caused TejBahadur to take shelter beneath the shed. He leaned, with his elbow placed on the boot of the car Raj would take on his lonesome trips away from the temple site and to his troubled mind it came as no consequence to find it open.

TejBahadur lifted it open, lighted a match stick and groped around at myriad things lying inside only to find a box containing two dozen of the small white marble statues of Sai Baba.

The secret of statues thus now known, a very perturbed devout hindu found himself in front of RajShekhar after a few days later begging for forgiveness and asking him to be relived of the services.

"I want to go to Nepal for Dassehara, Sahab, said TejBahadur,and accounts once settled, bidding well to all, the Nepali made his way back home, a very dejected, agnostic person. The man was worth his salt thought Raj, realizing much later, that the Nepali had not spoken a word of his discovery to anyone.

Small shrubs and wild growth could now be seen at the construction site. All that stood was the forty by six hundred feet marble platform, some six feet high, without steps to climb on. Vishwanath would often be seen sitting there in the company of a handful of locals, mainly the sarpanch* and the staff.

He continued with his Thursday prayers and distribution of prasadam*, quite unaware of RajShekhar's interaction and exchange of copies of the land documents with persons of money and influence.

Trapped in a situation, where his own wife and family mistrusted him, Vishwanath could not grasp what had transpired and what would, in near future. Raj was only awaiting the moment he could distance himself from him and the place. Period.

Father in law of the triumvirate was a very concerned man now with the entire happenings and worried about his daughters' fate, specially the wives of Raj and Vishwanath. After some consultations, he decided to travel to the temple site to bring the entire matter to an open family forum. So it passed that Mrutyunjay Prasad and his good driver left the city to cover some five hundred and eighty miles to the site on that fateful Sunday morning to reach the place by late night.

Frantic calls were made late in the night as the old man had not reached the destination well beyond the time. Absence of cell phone then and the remoteness made it more difficult for any communication to be effective.

Sunil Kumar's political connections though still hot, it was late in the morning that the news of the car crashing into a stationary twelve wheeled commercial vehicle was known. Both occupants dead. The sons-in-law rushed to the city to be with the grieving wives and rest of the family. In his death Mrutyunjay Prasad had at least brought about the reconciliation between his shattered daughter and Vishwanath.

RajShekhar knew he had to get back to the site to tie up the ends, to deal all aces if the objective had to be met, and a fortnight later he was seen back once again at his make shift office, going about the business as usual.

"Vishwanath should be back shortly." He told the staff, some faithful and the Sarpanch. The obvious query followed this time from tea vendor from the cross roads,

"Is the work on the temple going to start now that the rains have subsided?"asked the vendor. He had a lot to lose if the project did not culminate as perceived initially.

"Frankly", answered Raj," I am unable to see any light at the end of this dark tunnel of life. The recent developments have left me numb and speechless, I do not know what to make of it."

He stopped and after a short while said' "I had immense faith in Vishwanath and his spiritual contiguity towards Sai Baba."

He stopped again, trying to measure the impact on the listeners and continued, "but if what he claimed to be, that is conduit to Baba, a messenger, then he should have known of the calamity that was to befall on Mrutyunjay Prasad," said Raj in a slightly high-pitched voice.

"He could have made efforts to have the old man abort the journey".

With the exception of one or two, rest fell for the grossly inane argument. This proved to be the beginning of the end of Vishwanath's tryst with destiny.

Even today if one happens to travel on that high way, the marble platform surrounded by shrubs and bushes, uncared for, is a mute testimony of man's greed. RajShekhar sold the lands at a very high margin leaving Vishwanath a broken man to fend for himself.

So much for Sai.

Paakeeza

• Chapter 1 •

Axe Forgets, the Tree Remembers

Her world collapsed in a matter of a night.

Gauri was the fourth child of Durgaprasad. In all seven daughters were born every second year to Saraswati, persistent effort having failed to beget a male child. In spite of many abstruse remarks from the village folk or relatives, about the curse of not be getting a male child, husband and wife never really grudged or cursed the fate, but with equal care and affection, nurtured the girls, getting them married just after attaining puberty. This is a very common occurrence in villages of the entire Indian subcontinent. Importance to primary education is a very recent phenomenon.

The first three daughters were already married to fine young men engaged as small tradesmen. Durgaprasad had a decent job as a muneem* taking care of the petty accounts and allocating work to the handy boys at the estate of the extremely affluent local landlord. Each morning, Saraswati would be up very early and release the hens from the coop, get the food ready for the four girls, mother in law and her husband after serving them with piping hot tea. It was left to the eldest of the four to brush and tie up the thick black disheveled hair into neatly woven plaits." Go now and come back with a bundle each" the mother would say to the girls, tucking a chrysanthemum into their thick hair.

The firewood requirement for cooking was met from the bordering forest. No axe was ever used, no branch was ever broken and no animal ever hurt. No wonder then that the girls chirped like the birds and scurried around like the squirrels, collecting the fallen twigs and branches. Spirit of the forest is what they all had and little Gauri with her bow shaped eyebrows, long lashes and dove like eyes stood out as a beautiful forest fairy. The brown pupils strangely attracted and perhaps brought about some sensuous emotions. "The snake eyed one" her grandmother would say knowingly. Many mythical stories are woven around the mesmerizing eyes of the damsels to which fell prey the Gods, the demons and men alike.

On return, the girls would quickly finish eating and run to join the others to just sit and gossip or play some games. The most sought after game was the Hop-Scotch, a very popular backyard game in villages and towns alike. Gauri was adept at it and would emerge the winner on most days. A pattern of squares would be drawn on the ground, A flat stone would then be selected to be thrown into the square, taking precaution that the stone did not touch the border of any square. The contender then would hop on one leg, jumping from square to square. Both feet could not be put down unless the sequentially numbered squares that were adjoining each other.

Thus hopping the player would pick up the flat stone, go to the last square, hop around and turn. Throw the stone again and carry on. The player with the stone in hand, who could negotiate the squares first, would be the winner. Passers-by would take delight in observing the young damsels at play, all talking and giggling in unison till late in the dusk.

Festivals in India are the occasion when families get together, honour the old, indulge the relations and regale the young ones. The household of Durgaprasad was no different. Almost thrice a year the siblings of either Saraswati or Durgaprasad and of course the three daughters with their husbands in tow would descend and much would be the gaiety and celebrations.

Sankranti is one of the most auspicious festival for the Hindus, celebrated all over in a myriad of cultural forms. The Punjabis call it the Lohri, deep down south it's called Pongal and Sankranti. North easterners call it Maah Bihu and the most populace states of Bihar and UP call it the Kichadi, a mix of lentils and rice signifying a harvest festival when Sun begins his ascendency and entry into the northern hemisphere.

Thus it signifies an event wherein the Sun god seems to remind "tamaso ma jyothirgamaya – may you go to more light and not darkness". Wisdom, not ignorance. Sobriety and not intoxication. Unfortunately the very festival of the gods is often desecrated by the creation of the god's ambrosia—the soma rasa – the wine – the distilled country liquor.

Gauri had just about turned eleven this festive time. The generally quite home had turned into a cacophonic den with the daughters of Durgaprasad all giggling and talking to each other merrily while the sons in law along with Saraswati's four younger brothers, three wives and children milled around the couple in endless conversation and play. Every female member participated in making choice dishes while the men sat around playing cards and regaling themselves.

Come evening and the male members of the family would form into groups, the younger ones shying away from the elders to soak themselves with liquor. The youngest brother of Saraswati, a widower, would generally be sharing lighter moments with the girls.

"Are you planning to elope with one of the girls, Surya?", quizzed, Padma, the eldest of the wives of Saraswati's brothers, mirthfully, causing Surya to take his leering eyes away from Gauri. Vast age difference is what deterred

Saraswati in persuading her husband to give Gauri in marriage to her brother.

In many Muslim and Hindu societies in Africa, Asia and India, consanguineous marriages still are prevalent. This is not practiced now in Europe and other continents though History speaks of ancient Greece, where all rulers of Ptolemaic dynasty from Ptolomy II were married to brothers and sisters to keep the Ptolomic blood and the line of succession. There would be many political, socio-economic reasons to this type of union but the negative health effect caused by inbreeding are due to the expression of a rare dormant and detrimental gene that is inherited from common single shared ancestors. It is said to increase morbidity. Though a very controversial subject, nevertheless it is still practiced.

Surya, leaned against the trunk of the jack fruit tree, smoking and looked vaguely at the bright moon. The sort of make shift toilet was at one end of the compound surrounding the house, erected with the help of wooden posts and barbed wire. At the other end was the wicker gate. It was after 9pm and the family after a heavy festival dinner was preparing to sleep. The next day would be grueling work for the women. Huge preparation was needed to put together the food needed for the big gathering. Durgaprasad had invited some friends over for pre-festival lunch, mainly consisting of curried sheep meat and rice.

Just then Surya saw Gauri walk past to address the nature's call giving him a sheepish smile. Lost in deep thought, he just stood there, rooted to the ground, unaware of the lighted cigarette dangling from the fingers. His mind, cluttered with the images of the girl's mesmerizing eyes. He suddenly felt the sharp burning of the skin as the cigarette reached its end. Thoughts disrupted, he threw the butt down and saw the girl skip-running in her bright yellow long skirt and green blouse.

"Gauri,", called out Surya in a soft tone and beckoned the startled girl to trace her steps back to where he now stood. The large girth of the old tree almost hiding him from the view.

"What is it, uncle, I was about to go to bed" enquired the girl, coming near the man, her radiant face showing signs of anxiety. Without a spoken word the man pulled the girl near him, running his palm over the soft cheeks, looking deep into her eyes," nothing, I just wanted to buy you some nice bangles for the festival "said Surya, sliding his palm on the girl's chest, resting it just above the slight bulge. He was watching her intensely and finding no adverse emotions, proceeded to caress the bulge.

He could feel some hardening just below his palm, about the size of an orange pip. Thus encouraged, while his left palm rested on the chest of the girl, the right glided down to the well molded hips, moving in a circular motion. Gauri did not seem to mind this and stood still with muted interest, perhaps more inquisitive than aroused having occasionally seen her elder sisters, mirthfully giggling, while their husbands engaged in similar playful acts.

Medical journals report though that the response to stimulation can be intense at the onset of puberty in girls generally between the age of ten and thirteen. This took all about quarter of an hour before Gauri extricated herself, nodding and walking swiftly away towards the house." Do not mention this to anyone, I will accompany you to the forest for the wood in the morning," Surya had whispered.

Next day at the forest while the girls were busy collecting the fallen branches, almost similar act followed. Surya was not a compulsive pedophile, but Gauri had aroused in him long dormant urge for the stimulation, causing him to want to indulge in an incestuous relationship, as happens generally and in most cases within immediate family. There was much activity in the house as guests had come for the pre-festival get-together, mostly Durgaprasad's friends. Surya did not join the revelry but kept aloof, lying on a mat contemplating his next move. The unused and ram shackled forest guardroom flashed in his mind repeatedly.

The nearest town was just some two kilometers away and was serviced by private, as well as, state owned buses apart from autos to ferry people up and down from small hamlets dotted about the district. The large shops selling household goods, the ready-made garments and the bank was not what the folks used to travel to town for, but for the fancy goods shops and the pawn brokers who generally did brisk business with them. The three cinema halls were also frequented, specially, when they screened the family melodramas.

It was quite late in the evening when Surya returned bringing four different coloured bangles, delectable sweets and savories and laid them open for Durgaprasad's mother to distribute. Bangles for the four girls and the rest for all to enjoy. He kept away the dainty bottle of perfume for later use.

"Let us go away to the forest when all have their afternoon nap, I have a surprise for you" said Surya to a much amused Gauri who nodded in immediate agreement as any child would, faced with the prospects of merriment. That afternoon both slipped away in silence.

Forest spread on the other side of the state high way bordering the hamlet. Unchecked deforestation had deprived the elephants and deer inhabiting the area, to seek fodder deeper and only the monkeys, squirrels, rodents and reptiles of snake family ruled the roost. Most fortunate were the descendants of the Hindu God Hanuman, believed to be reincarnation of Lord Shiva in the form of a monkey on Earth, a symbol of strength, perseverance and devotion.

The private bus owners would send sacks full of marginally spoiled fruits to be fed to them. The creatures, all in well-knit groups, under the command of an aging patriarch would wait for the vehicles to pass. Great was the sight and greater was the delight this would provide to young and the old alike. Gauri's face lighted with delight as she crossed the road to enter the much ventured forest she knew so well.

The heat of the open suddenly gave way to cool breeze and the numerous trees dotting the thorn scrub forest sheltered the Blue winged Parakeet and the likes of wood pecker, grass bird, swallows, mynahs and some more. She knew her trees well and loved them in sort of semi reverence for protection they provided to the creatures and firewood to the humans, as well as, delectable honey from the numerous bee hives hanging from the thick branches. Gauri could even point out which of the Soapnut, Pongamia or the Neem tree they used to hang the rope swings from. There was an abundance of custard apple trees growing wild, fruiting in season.

A little distance away, walking through the winding well-trodden foot path was the Baniyan tree with multiple roots hanging from its branches. It must have stood guard in the forest for many decades now and was known for sheltering in its natural recess at the very root of the large trunk, the stone image of a hooded serpent. The place and the stone were splattered with vermillion, turmeric and people worshiped in the hope that veneration would make the serpent, protect and not harm the devotee.

Many myths are built around the serpent, through centuries of evolving civilization. Ancient Mesopotamians believed that snake was immortal as it sheds its skin and appears in a new guise, several times in its life cycle. Gauri bent and folded her hands in reverence in front of the stone image and taking a small pinch of the vermillion applied it on her forehead, just between those mesmerizing eyes. The added extra sparkle in her face only further aggravated Surya's adrenal glands.

The forest department usually has a room or two constructed in the open grassland area for the guards who keep a watch on the forest produce that is auctioned away each year. The venue changes and the staff is shifted from place to place. General apathy towards maintenance results in small structure becoming dilapidated and the growth of moss and creepers cause further deterioration. Devoid of trees, the tenement and the area surrounding, finds no village folk in and around the vicinity. Grassland also homes many varied coloured butterflies which feeds on the nectar from the flowers blooming on host plants. There were many species. Gauri ran behind a blue Mormon as if to catch it and slipped, her foot stumbling against a growth of rattle weed.

"Are you hurt". Screamed Surya. She nodded in negation and brushed aside her long skirt standing up. "Let's go, we will go and sit under the shade of the room" saying so Surya led her inside the room, breaking a branch of Pongamia covered with leaves to sweep the floor with.

"Here try this, you will smell better than any of your friends," said Surya bringing out the tiny perfume bottle for Gauri. "Even the jasmine you string to your hair will not compare" saying so he dabbed a little on his middle finger and rubbed it across her chest. Intuitively Gauri lifted her loose pink blouse to *breath in the fragrance of the strong, long lasting extract of cepes and tuberose. None had ever given* her a more endearing gift thought the girl as Surya unable to contain himself seeing her bared waist slid both the palms beneath her blouse and caressed her tenderly, till he felt the familiar hardening.

Gauri did not seem to mind this. It could have been the inquisitiveness or the simple fact that even infants respond to stimulation and the search in the subject has it that the desire grows from birth and is intense at the onset of puberty. Expression of interest varies from muted response to spontaneity, thereby increasing the risk manifolds for the girl child.

How so ever Darwin may have described the process of evolution, the species would not have survived without this motivational aspect. Thirst for water and food motivates the organism to consume, or else it will perish. Similarly the motivation for copulation drives the organism, resulting in off-springs. Devoid of this the species would be extinct.

However any abuse manifests itself into physiological and psychological disasters.

Surya, with heavier breathing and faster palpitation, had now turned the flushed face of the girl towards his own, and taking her lower lip into his own began kissing her feverishly while his hands continued to feel the chest. The sensation was totally foreign to Gauri as she felt her muscles tensing up. It was then that Surya slid his hand on her thighs and began unknotting the string holding her skirt to the waist. The reflex was quick, as Gauri held tight at the knot. Surya still kissing her as if to silence any protest entwined his fingers into hers and pushed the hand away, slowly releasing her lips.

"What is the matter, do you feel shy?" he questioned her. Gauri took her eyes away and tried to break loose, anxiety written large on her face. His grip tightened. Holding her from the back with one hand he lifted her skirt, exposing the crotch covered with fine vellus hair, pinning her legs down with his own. In a moment Surya was on her. Holding both legs apart he tried to enter her, to be confronted with the natural resistance of a fluid less passage. He lustily thrust himself, half way through as the girl shrieked in pain, begging him to stop.

Surya continued, repeatedly pulling out and re-entering her in spite of the growing protests and obvious agony. There prevails a general misconception in the mind of men, be it a rapist, pedophile or a sodomizer, that during copulation, more forceful the thrust, a female tends to enjoy more. Nothing can be far from scientific truth. The act is, in all likelihood the desire of men to portray dominance.

With a sudden movement Surya penetrated fully amidst a piercing shriek from Gauri who was sweating all over profusely now. It is then after couple of thrusts that he ejaculated with a heavy grunt and slowly withdrew, releasing the girls thighs, when he noticed some white mucous like fluid ooze out with traces of blood. Surya quickly stole a glance at her, to notice the face and general appearance, giving out all obvious signs of diminished alertness and tremor. The internal lacerations caused by the thrusts of the Oedipal love making was resulting in a crimson flow of the blood now. Gauri sobbed unabated, holding her head, in between spasmodic cough and bouts of nausea.

Surya wrapped his left arm around the girl's back and helped her sit, all the while entreating her to quieten down. Gauri had doubled over, bending the head on to her raised knees, covering her face, sobbing uncontrollably.

'Listen Gauri, I did not know that it will pain you like so, have you not seen others do it around the house in the dead of the night? It is great fun. I do not know what happened to you and why you have bled. This does not happen and I promise you it never will again" said Surya trying to sooth the girl's nerves and setting her up for future adventures.

"Yes, it never will again" screamed Gauri, suddenly shaking herself free with all the strength she could gather and ran out of the room as if possessed. Surya not anticipating this, followed behind only to see Gauri tumble again beyond the holy tree, fall down, crashing on her knees. He once again helped her up only to see a torn skirt and a badly bruised knee bleeding and plastered with mud.

"See what you are doing to yourself, please calm down" pleaded Surya trying to brush the soil away from the bleeding wound. Gauri, finding herself, totally exhausted offered no resistance as he guided her to the stone bench near the big tree. Surya himself now was covered in perspiration and fatigue. Man's body chemistry changes after orgasm, depleting his muscle energy, leading to a roll over and snore.

Gauri sat, looking away from Surya, painfully aware now of the full implication of what had transpired.

"I am going to tell everyone what you did to me today" she said, slightly composed, still painful and agonizingly confused, still looking away.

Surya remained quiet, contemplating, perhaps sensing an opportunity in the situation to turn the events to his advantage, not in the least giving a thought to the pain physically and mentally, the girl was going through. The long lasting effect, manifesting itself into varieties of psychological harm, is manifolds, if the perpetrator of the crime is a relation. Worldwide, incestual rape has proved to be one of the most extreme forms of childhood trauma.

"come, let us go home Gauri" said Surya softly. "No one is ever going to believe you, including your father and what about your friends? You will only be a laughing stock for them if they hear of this. There is no harm done. You will feel fine in a few hours. Eat heartily and go to sleep tonight"

They walked in silence and were at the hand pump by the road side in a matter of quarter of an hour. Gauri washed, splattering her face with water. All she wanted now was a bath to clean herself up. Her mind mulling over the whole situation. Though still eleven, Gauri could simulate in her mind the reprisal, the stigma and the hostility towards a female in such a situation, specially, in small towns and villages. Most of the cases of rape remain unreported, even to the family, because of lack of response and negative attribution of motives by the near ones.

Gauri walked home with Surya in tow, in total silence ignoring even the friendly gestures of the passersby.

"Where were you both, did not see you around with the others today" enquired the old lady of the house, looking sleepily through her thick glasses, the pince-nez hanging loose on her broad nose. Gauri simply walked by, leaving Surya to satiate the grandmother's concern out of loneliness and being generally ignored, as is the case in all households.

"Oh! we were just at the road side, watching people scurry around with other folks, mother," said Surya and hurried away, behind Gauri, to find the conclave of women gathered around in the courtyard dressed in all finery, giggling and talking almost all together with betel nut juice dribbling slightly out of the side of their lips, unaware of the intrusion.

Padma the eldest, of the sister in laws of Saraswati, mother of three children was the only one with eyes on Gauri. One intense look and she could sense something amiss. Padma was President of one of the thrift groups formed by the nationalized banks, Grameen* branch, to encourage savings and enterprise among women folk. Her husband, the watch maker though not appreciative, minded his own, sensing the marginal local clout she wielded.

Surya smiled at them and traced his steps to gather a straw mat to sooth his wobbly limbs. No trace of remorse.

No one took notice of Padma's absence, such is the effect of idle gossip that overpowers the senses in a gathering at the melancholic homestead of country folks at festive times. Padma found the child standing, staring at nothing on the roof top. Unheard she stepped, beside a very startled Gauri, holding the child's cheeks in her palms, she questioned,

"what is the matter? I find you so withdrawn and out of sorts", only to find very moistened eyes, bereft of all the mesmerism they were known for.

Amidst Gauri's sobbing and broken narration it was not difficult for Padma to gather the significance of the entire happening of that fateful day. That night Padma slept with the girls, regaling them with the stories built around the antics of the elephant headed god. Her mind absorbed with the course of action needed to be ensured for the safety of the traumatized child. Any unwanted pregnancy would be catastrophic and only put the child to social ridicule, as well as, prove disastrous for the entire family.

The best way out was to consult and medicate the girl and make way for the next course of action, decided Padma. Festival day was still one day away and there was little time to waste.

"I am taking all the children to the Temple of Lord Ganesha", declared Padma at the morning tea and asked the girls to hurry up with the routine. No one was surprised knowing the determination and presumptuous nature of the lady, so native to her. There was a scurry of activity and in a span of less than an hour all the girls were out in the court yard, brightly dressed and raring to go. Happy at the prospect of the bus ride to the town. Gauri was not seen in the company.

Padma had taken her to the prayer corner in the house and both were bending, hands folded in front of the plethora of bright pictures of Hindu Gods.

"Lord Vinayaka*, you are the only recourse now, pray, help this child in this most testing time" saying so bowing in front of the picture of Lord Ganesha – the Vighnanashak*-remover of all obstacles, Padma took the wrist of the girl to guide her and joined the children waiting in great expectation, along with the elders.

It was a merry scene to see a score of girls along with the matronly ladies hurrying towards the road. Padma had asked the woman from the neighborhood to accompany them. All along, Gauri kept to herself holding on to the aunt, who had taken the precaution of letting the group know that the girl was unwell and may have to see the doctor once in town.

The Temple was situated at one side of the town, a good half an hour of walk. Padma bought for all the girls some candy floss and salted peanuts to munch while they trotted on to the shrine, holding hands. There will be sweetened rice, laced with cashew nuts and raisins for the devotees, distributed by the priest's assistants, after offering the same to the Lord. Children always looked forward to it and sometimes were able to extract extra portion from the friendly attendees. Once at the temple, the group left the footwear outside and stood deep in reverence with folded hands, each seeking favours.

Gauri's thoughts were elsewhere and her face, totally devoid of any emotions, was still betraying her agony. She silently ate and stood looking at the rabbits kept by the temple authorities in an enclosure as an added attraction for the conglomeration of devotees flocking the place.

Suddenly there was a flurry of activity inside the enclosure, the large grey toned male was furiously shaking his hind pinning down a doe in the act of copulation, leaving the small young ones and sundries to shy away from the vicinity. Gauri stared wide eyed at the happenings. In a short span of time, the male tipped over on his side and remained immobile as if dead. It was very relaxed. Animal instincts, varies from humans to the lowly ants. The doe rose in a frenzy, catching the neck of her tormentor and bit hard to leave two spots of blood smears on the fur. The doe simply had acted in accordance to the basic instincts of the species. The incidence however reminded Gauri of her own agonizing moments, as she turned way to join the group. The male tiptoed to a corner to get a blissful nap.

Padma guided the group back to the town center near the bus stand, close to the municipal park where the local body had installed couple of swings, slides and merry go rounds.

"Shakuntala, here take this and get them all something solid to eat and lemon soda, you get excellent idlis* at the eatery opposite the park, or whatever they fancy" handing over some cash to the neighbour, Padma continued,

"we shall be back in an hour or so, I am taking Gauri to the doctor, she seems to have some fever or to the mendicant to tie up a talisman".

Children were happy at the prospect of the popping cool drink and so was Shakuntala, getting a chance to be out of her non-descript life.

Padma 's close friend was employed at the clinic of Dr. Snehlatha. R.M.P., practicing general medicine. The paucity or the cost involved in regular medical studies has resulted in state being empowered to allow registered medical practitioners, having qualified under integrated degrees, not conventional medical studies, to practice and prescribe allopathic medicines. What this has not factored in, is the intensity and rigors of modern conventional studies so central inspite of technological developments to discharge proper medical care. However, this relaxation has lead to primary medical care to millions of rural India, by not fully qualified professionals. This has had its implications.

Padma explained the situation to the doctor and her friend in isolation taking care to avoid family scandal. Dr Snehlatha examined the scared child to find the lacerations and obvious injuries to the genitals and suggested intake of DES, the "morning after pill" a post-coital contraceptive. This medication has been in use widely, having some side effects and often causes forced menstruation in prepubescent minors.

All will be well thought Padma, when the group reached back to the village and next two days were spent in celebrations. At the end, all the relations departed one by one. Padma pulled Gauri's mother to a side and whispered,

"I feel in my bones that this girl will soon come off age, that may be the reason for her sudden change in behavior. Do call us when that happens for the rituals."

Saying so, she bid farewell to all, patting the three girls on the head affectionately. It is a custom in some Indian communities and sections of the societies to welcome the onset of puberty as a joyous function.

Such were the circumstances in the household of Durgaprasad.

Gauri remained withdrawn and avoided all company, expect at meal times, just picking at her food. After-effects of forceful sexual encounter can manifest itself in many forms. Saraswati noticed her daughter taking bath often during the day and discussed this with her husband, who brushed aside the matter speculating that this could just be a temporary phase. Trauma of the sort, Gauri was undergoing caused some to take baths often, as if wanting to cleanse oneself repeatedly. Sometimes, she would be seen suddenly sobbing without apparent cause. This can have serious Psychological impact too.

The situation was incomprehensible to one and all in the family and neighborhood.

It is in this phase of the girls life that she felt a sharp pain in the pelvic area, one evening and the bleeding started. A very disturbed and painful Gauri ran to her mother who casually explained about the facts of body behavior and life thereafter. Function was quickly arranged and few relatives were again at the dwelling of Durgaprasad. On the fifth day Gauri was ritually dressed in sort of a bridal attire as is the custom. She showed no apparent interest in the procedure, nor in the gifts that were showered on her. Her face lit up only when Padma showed up with her husband in tow, talking loudly, all at once and all the while with everyone present there. What she carefully avoided was, mentioning that Suryanarayan was also there.

The fare was simple, but satiated all and after the exchange of betel leaf, nut and coconut, relations and guests started departing, blessing Gauri and taking leave of the matriarch, younger ones and the couple.

All was quite now and Padma settled down,alongside her watch maker husband with Saraswati and Durgaprasad for a quite and pre meditated dialect.

"What are you planning for Gauri now, sister" asked Padma,directing her glance towards Durgaprasad. He had raised all his seven daughters with care, equal affection and it only mattered to him that they have a blissful married life and many grand children to regale himself once retire.

"I would have married her off, even if I had to take a loan at heavy interest rate, if there was a younger one born after Surya" exclaimed the man, thinking of the expenses involved if Gauri had to be married now. Padma and her husband were dumb struck, never expecting a reaction so close to what they had conceived, within a short time of the mis-happening.

"Why do you not consider giving her to Surya himself" said Padma and waited to see the reactions.

"We are four of us and sharing a common house. Father left us with enough land. We shall write off a fourth to your daughter and construct a new house for her too, what do you say, matter of age may be just eight to nine years more than desired?" proposed Saraswati's brother.

The offer was in keeping with the tradition of consanguineous marriage prevalent. Durga's aching bones could ask for nothing better." Anyway, let's ask my daughter, "said Durgaprasad, knowing fully well that none of his children ever would and will stand contrary to his wishes. Surya was still around with a package under his arms near the tree.

All settled, they decided to call Gauri and put the proposition to her, less that more a dictate, as the way of life is.

"How are you feeling now" asked Padma moving her palm softly on the girls head," now you are a woman and should think of settling down in marriage" she continued. Gauri just looked vacantly at her mother, not grasping or detached at the subject of conversation and shifted her eyes vacantly at her favourite aunt. Durgaprasad, now fully convinced of the advantages, was eager to broach and close the deal.

'Little one," said he," we want you to marry Suryanarayan, and lead a happy life like your elder sisters. I and your mother have agreed for this alliance" saying so he slipped the package Surya had silently passed on.

Never had the couple seen any of their daughters in a more repulsively agitated manner than what they saw of Gauri that day. She simply jumped up in all her finery, kicked the package and screamed, hitting her forehead, sharply with her palm," I do not want to have anything to do with him nor do I want to marry" saying so and giving Padma a sharp look through her blood shot eyes, Gauri ran out of the house. Her each pore sweating and shivering as if possessed. Everything came to a standstill and everyone one was dumb founded.

Whatever the circumstances, whatever the logic!

AXE FORGETS, BUT THE TREE REMEMBERS.

• Chapter 2 •

Tommorow Never Dies

Shankar had this strange habit of scratching his left leg with the right foot. Not because it itched but some force of habit developed in early childhood, when he ran away from home and took refuge with Shyamala and Krishnadas in their sprawling bunglow and large stretch of cultivable lands. Faced with an awkward situation some scratch their head, few rub the nose. Shankar was different.

The couple were in their late sixties. Their only child, a son, an engineer by profession had after marriage, sought transfer to Darjeeling where the Hydro-electricity project was in its inception. Shankar himself was now over thirty. A failed marriage and a young daughter separated from him now for over two years, meant nothing as Shankar continued with his waywardness while enjoying the patronage of the couple as their handyman and major domo.

"I have not seen you around since dinner last night, where have you been?" chided Krishnadas, wanting to hear some lame excuse for his absence till late afternoon. Shyamala for one, was particular that the bandicoot, as she addressed him, was well fed. The couple continued to care for him for over two decades now.

"You know that single horned one is about to deliver and she can have convulsions any time, you cannot fool around and let the calf also perish along with its mother, what have we done to deserve a good for nothing fellow like you" shouted the old man, feeling the palm of his wife over his as if to suggestively sooth him down.

Shyamala understood the outburst of her husband who treated the cow as his own progeny and knew too well the repercussions of Shankar not being around altogether. She slowly walked away to the kitchen to come out with a large plate full of rice and curry and placed it down. Krishnadas as his anger diminished, smiled knowingly at his wife and continued with his betel nut chewing. Shankar, his head lowered, silently ate the food.

There was regular work for four to five labourers every day. Two crops of paddy had to be cultivated each year other than chili, long red variety, was grown throughout the year and spread on the roof top to dry and stored. Krishnadas waited for the upswings in commodity prices as keeps happening at the wholesale markets and dispose of the dried, pungent spice packed in gunny bags. Till recently, the major crop contributing to the regular income consisted of the spice, paddy getting used up as a staple for the whole year.

Almost four times a year Shankar had to take the paddy to the rice mill to obtain rice as well as the husk. Some sacks of paddy were kept away for sale during festive season to manage the extra expenditure or to invest in gold. Husk was equally important as a supplementary diet for the cattle, like a booster mixed with groundnut cake, left-over food and water with a dash of salt.

The climatic conditions, soil and the temperature was very suitable for fruit bearing varieties, the likes of Jamun*, Guavas and Mango trees. Gooseberry was a recent addition to the area as Ayurvedic Pharma companies had started promoting the sour tasting fruit as a cash crop. The sales of natural and time tested paste, an amalgamation of

Gooseberry, some spices and honey has seen a phenomenal growth in sales in recent years. Established organizations, as well as upstarts, wanting a market share in the organic and medicinal preparations were feverishly promoting the cultivation of gooseberry plants.

Six years ago, Krishnadas had obtained the free saplings from one such group with a buy back guarantee at the prevailing market rate. This year was to be the first year of harvest as minimum maturity period was fixed before yield would be taken for pulping. The field officers came regularly to take stock of the situation.

"Another fortnight and please arrange the laborers to pluck the berry direct from the trees, without letting them fall on the ground and have them packed in wicker baskets for transportation and weighment at the collection center please" the field officer had advised informing at the same time, that cash would be paid by the regional office the next day.

On the fixed day, a score of young boys were called from the neighbouring village to climb the trees, pluck the berries and lower the small collection bags to Krishnadas and Shankar below. This was then poured gently into the baskets. All counted, some thirty baskets were ready, stitched with rough cloth cover and secured in the waiting tempo to be transported at day break. "Load is not bad, from one hundred and fifty trees for the first harvest, dear" said Krishnadas addressing his apprehensive wife.

"Let's see what we get in hand after adjustment of the plantation cost and expenditure. After all, we also waited for six full years for the yield" replied Shyamala. Apart from labour, cost for planting, plucking and drying, the chilies, the hot spice, always left a handsome earning for them year after year. Horticulture and specially Gooseberry, was totally alien to the people and the place. Now some acreage was also sliced away from the area allocated by the couple towards the regular crop. This worried Shyamala, though she camouflaged the feeling very effectively not to pass on any worries to her husband.

Krishnadas along with Shankar, departed early in the morning to reach the product at the collection center, some three hour's drive towards the big metro. Once inside the large shed, the baskets were unloaded near an array of tables mounted with large metal trays having a hole at the far corner of one side. The rejects would be dropped through the hole into a collect bin for the farmer to take back. There were already three loads before Krishnadas's.

The first load was taken for segregation with two workers doing the job on each side. The farmer had brought roughly five hundred kilograms of Gooseberry and at the end of the process some seventy kilograms were rejected to the despair of the man. This itself had taken roughly four hours. It was past noon when the supervisor called in the load of Krishnadas, who by now was in quite a disturbed state, mentally and physically, not having eaten a morsel from the time they had left home.

"Please sit and rest here, I will attend to the work "said Shankar, handing over two bananas and a packet of biscuits. He also had managed to get some water sachets from road side shop a little distance away from the collection center. The process had begun and lasted till late afternoon and at the end of it three hundred kilograms had to be repacked in ten baskets to take back. This was almost half of the harvest.

Krishnadas was devastated and all through the journey back, kept to himself.

"What do we do with this left over berries, Appa?".

Shankar's quarry fell on deaf ears as the aging and bent over man sat with his head tilted to a side pulling at the bidi, occasionally almost smokeless.

"Are you listening? We have to find a way to dispose them before we reach home and face Amma" Shankar prodded on, his own face showing signs of distress and anxiety.

The tempo rattled on, negotiating the craters in the tar road recently leveled, unmindful of pitfalls in human life.

"Let us go to the market yard at the next junction and see if we can find means to salvage the situation" said the old man almost inaudible and glancing away from the baskets and his man Friday. Shankar asked the tempo to divert towards small town called Gutti, where market yard was situated some two miles from home.

The Big Brands entering the retail sector or the firms encouraging farmers to grow specific agricultural produce were insensitive to farmer's plight about the graded rejects. This was to gradually give rise to contract farming with its own pitfalls in time to come.

The throw away price obtained at the market yard along with what the Pharma company had given, Krishnadas found to his dismay that, he had made a loss of couple of hundreds after taking all costs into consideration.

"What are we to do now" was the only dialogue between the old couple that night. Krishnadas, turned his head on the soiled pillow and was far away in deep slumber caused by fatigue and distress.

The same routine continued for a fortnight, with no or near-to-nil earnings coming his way. Krishnadas, was spending more of his melancholic time at the road side tea shop in the company of strangers passing that way. Shankar would come and take the old man back home if it was late. Desperation and despondence written large on his face.

"We have to harvest the next batch of berries in two days. Shall I engage the labourers?" proposed Shankar. "they have not been paid for the previous harvest," he reminded, looking away. Krishnadas only nodded and continued to trudge home wards. He knew that whatever will be received from the sale at the collection center will go towards the accumulated labour charges.

Next evening again, Krishnadas was at the tea shop. The owner was in know of general farming conditions prevailing in the region. Crops would be destroyed if there was untimely rain fall. Cyclonic effects would render the standing crop of Jowar, Paddy or Sugar Cane to fall flat, the drought results in huge production losses. Tea shops are generally the center of village gossip, as well as the meeting venue for all and sundry.

"I heard others talk about the tall promises made by the company in making you plant the trees and the pittance they give you now" said Ranga, the tea shop owner, with a genuine feel.

"You are right, I should have stuck to traditional crops but for the smooth talking representative of theirs who is nowhere to be seen now. It is more to do with rejects just because of the size of the berry," continued Krishnadas," What can anyone do with god given fruits? No one has control over that." Lamented the man

"Look every night just when I am about to close, a vegetable lorry comes for the tea. They fill the thermos and take it for the long overnight journey. I have heard them mention about the huge market yard and it appears every variety in varying sizes is offloaded there for the consumption by the huge population there as well for export." Said Ranga, adding further that he would be happy to discuss the matter with the driver if the old man could send across the sample that night.

So it came to pass, sample was sent through Shankar. Subsequently it was arranged that the lorry would take the Gooseberry load along with Shankar to the Mega market yard. Narain, the driver was ready to give all help and assistance for an agreed transportation charge. Belonging to the same caste plays a great role in arranging business deals and marriages in Indian country side. Similar was the case with all three. Krishnadas, the driver and the handy man.

The attempt at selling the Gooseberries at the large market yard proved very beneficial for the old man and soon the driver was solely managing the transaction. Neatly folded receipt along with the cash was handed over to him at the tea shop by Narain on his way back every week and soon a very strong relationship was forged between them.

There always is an opportunity in adversity.

The Pharma company took objection to this, however there was nothing that they could do to stop the transaction in absence of a firm commitment on paper and also they themselves had not adhered to a fair price and fair play policy. The realization came much later to them as the time passed by and as the story unfolds.

Earnings from the Gooseberry sales and yield from the newly acquired robust cows was sufficient to do away with the chilly crop which involved extensive labour. Shankar found more and more time on his hands. Thus began his involvement with the other natives, fond of slipping away to the shack at the outskirt where ample country liquor was brewed, bottled and sold.

Shyamala was the one to notice the waywardness in Shankar's otherwise regular routine and behavior. Few words with the regular farm hands and she was wiser to the happenings.

"You know, Shyamala, I think we should stop the chilly plantation and instead plant Guava trees, specially the Allahabad variety. Gooseberry and Guava will ensure handsome returns every season. Paddy can continue. Our dependence on labour will decrease and we can relax at this age." Krishnadas explained to his wife one lazy afternoon. Shyamala saw reasonable sense in the proposal.

"What will you do with the cows, they need good care, don't they?" interrupted the lady, wanting to draw her husband closer to the matter troubling her mind about Shankar.

"Why, Shankar will take care of that, maybe with one young lad in tow. Don't you think?" asked the old man, expecting a positive response. That was it.

"That good for nothing fellow?, he is not to be trusted with anything these days, he has started going to the country liquor shop with the other hooligans. It is time you did something to tie him down, or else I will throw him out." Krishnadas knew his wife well enough to argue further. He did notice though, that Shankar when he came in would stagger a bit. Shyamala however put his plate filled with food by way of same affection and concern.

Hybrid Gooseberry ends fruiting by the onset of winter. Plants need less moisture thereafter. This was the right time to prepare the pits for plantation, fill them with manure, cover them with fallen leaves and cow excreta, for the natural metabolism to create the perfect nourishment for new plants at the onset of monsoon. Krishnadas did just that, keeping a constant eye on Shankar.

"He is like a son to us, with an unfortunate marriage. We would like him to settle down with a sprightly girl. Was what old man told Narain, his driver friend, later that week at the tea shop. "We do not care if she is from a poor household and cannot afford the expenses, we shall manage it."

Narain needed no more prompting. He was thinking of Durga, his childhood friend, and the daughters born to him year after year.

Tomorrow never dies.

• Chapter 3 •

Women Are Chattels

About six hundred pits were made ready for the mango saplings of Benishan variety, all filled with cow dung, covered with paddy stalks and fallen leaves to retain moisture. Sure way to encourage growth of earth worms, natures best species to convert organic matter into very fertile manure. Another three months and saplings could be put in place thought Krishnaprasad, looking at the neatly done rows of pits. He had arranged for saplings from a known nursery nearby.

Deviating from his normal routine, Narain shaved and bathed at the public facility near the market, dressed and drove away with a sack of fresh vegetables and a large packet of sweets. It was around noon that he changed the tracks and moved alongside the forested hamlets. Familiar road to his friend's house.

Durgaprasad's joy was unbounded to see his friend Narain, who came shouting his name, sack on his broad shoulders and the box of sweets in his hand.

"Look, Saraswati, the bandicoot has come at last" called Durga at the top of his voice while half hugging and half helping his friend in offloading the heavy sack.

Saraswati too was delighted to see the good friend of her husband after a lapse of over three years. Last she had seen him was at a wedding where husband and wife had gone.

"Please take a seat, Anna*, where have you been so long and how is my sister?" she enquired in a single breath, handing Narain a glass of water, who gulped it down swiftly and sat down smiling.

"All that later, tell me where are the little ones?" putting the glass away he asked about the girls while handing over the box of sweets and gesturing towards the vegetable sack. "Got some stuff for you from the market."

"The girls would be back from the forest soon, they are not anymore the little ones you talk about, specially your favourite, Gauri." Said Durgaprasad cheerfully. No better way to open the subject thought Narain.

The friends talked for some time very intimately, while Saraswati kept busy with preparing extra rice and fish curry laced with tamarind paste and spices, a dish very commonly enjoyed by all in their community. The strong aroma of the spices filled the whole neighborhood.

There was sound of the stacks of fire wood being thrown down and some chattering outside. The youngest was to rush in first shrieking, "What have you made, Ma." And then seeing a stranger stopped in her steps and glanced shyly at Narain.

"Don't you remember Narain mama*?" questioned Saraswati.

"Come sit beside me," said Narain, affectionately pulling the child towards him in an embrace and planting a kiss on the child's cheek. While Gauri walked in along with the other two siblings. Her eyes effortlessly mesmerizing the onlooker.

"Ah, this should be Gauri, "exclaimed Narain.

The girl now around fourteen was happy to see Narain. Someone not of the blood but with a close affinity towards the family, with no strings attached.

The most cruel and gruesome experience had left her with the usually associated post-traumatic stress behaviour. Durgaprasad was often perplexed at Gauri's sudden angry outbursts at seemingly petty matters and general withdrawal from friends, family and events. Sometimes he would find her extremely clingy with some, like Padma or Saraswati. His simple mind could not fathom the reason for the change in his otherwise beautiful and sprightly daughter.

Gauri was delighted to see Narain, associated in her memory with trips to fair grounds and all the gifts he used to shower the girls with, whenever he came visiting his friend and the family but that was some time back when he did not own the lorry, later bought second hand.

"Why, it is you, mama* said Gauri, coming and sitting beside the man who put his palm affectionately on her bountiful, thick, black hair, patting and blessing her. Saraswati too joined the conversation having put the rice to cook. The talk centered around all the daughters of Durgaprasad. Their family problems and general happenings around them.

Saraswati had asked Gauri to tend to the fire and cooking. If not schooling, this was one aspect all the elder girls had learnt from their mother and were deft at dishing out a good meal and keeping the house spotlessly clean. The basic training, a must in rural or urban Indian households. A necessity too as girls once married, were required to engage themselves in household work generally comprising of aging and demanding in laws and scores of siblings of the husband.

Gauri came out of the kitchen wiping her hands, to announce that food was ready and laid out.

"Come Abba, bring mama, both of you and sisters have lunch while it is hot." she announced, half looking at Narain who seemed very pleased with the idea of a hot meal with his friend and the family after a lapse of a long time. His mind was occupied with other matters but all in good time he thought.

The Tamarind, in this lovely fish curry, really gives it a tangy flavor to be eaten with hot boiled rice. Narain was ravenous after the long drive. It did not take him long to gulp down the spicy, aromatic food. Gauri got up to serve more to both her father and the guest with Saraswati chiding the girl to serve Narain a big helping of rice and curry. While bending down to serve, the long scarf covering her chest, slipped down much to the delight of the younger ones who could not stop giggling even as their mother tried in vain to silence them. Narain could not help noticing that the girl had come of age.

After the sumptuous meal both friends reclined on straw mats, under the shade of the large Jack fruit tree. Smoking and talking about life in general. From the Gilli-danda * days to now, each having respective responsibility and chores to attend to but the bonding was evident.

Sun was sliding silently behind the tree, throwing a radiant orange glow on the broad leaves of the jackfruit tree, when Narain got up and started pacing around, dangling a half burnt Gold Flake, the small one, by his lips.

"You know Durga, he started speaking in a soft voice," Your girl, Gauri, seems very strange to me as if there are two different humans in the same shell of human body. Sometimes very cheerful and radiant and at times very withdrawn and deep in thought. Have you noticed this strange mood swings of hers?"

Just when Narain finished asking this, Saraswati came out with the girls who were looking forward to a game of some sort with the friends or looking forward for a day with the family friend.

"Yes, I have noticed the behavior too," answered Durga, "Let us talk about that later." He stopped short as the wife and the girls came nearer. He primarily had no clue as to the state of mind of his daughter or the causes of it. He associated the mood swings to the child having attained puberty. That evening the girls getting into the front of the truck along with Durgaprasad, went to the nearby temple of the local deity, while Saraswati and Gauri accompanied the family standing at the back. Joy was unbounded for the first ever truck ride the girls had enjoyed.

Narain decided to spend that night at his friends place and when the girls had gone to bed, the two friends along with Saraswati sat around, chatting and popping betel nuts into their mouths.

"I have a dear friend of our own community about an hour's drive away". Started Narain opening up the subject of the alliance.

"He owns a large track of land with fruit trees and is also going to expand his mango orchard shortly", he continued sensing the interest Saraswati was taking in his narration, "they have a married son residing elsewhere because of job. The whole affair is managed by this adopted son Shankar on whom both the husband and wife dote". Durgaprasad now was fully drawn into what his friend was saying and stole a glance at his wife, who acknowledged and asked,

"What is it you are hinting at, Anna?" she quizzed.

"It is Shankar they want to get married to a nice girl" said Narain to let the matter sink in slowly before he could get to details. Now the interest of the couple had risen to the desired level and the friend continued,

"Shankar is a widower, and has total confidence of the couple, they would take care of the total expenditure and also assure that some part of the land will be written off to the girl who is married to this adopted son of theirs. I was thinking of our Gauri", said Narain and waited for the reaction. Now the couple looked at each other deeply.

"We can go and see Krishnadas and Shyamala, if you will tomorrow itself, when I get back "added the friend looking alternatively at the husband and the wife. Narain knew well the precarious position of finances and the difficulties with which Durgaprasad was managing the large household. So the night passed. Marrying off young girls to much older or a widower is very prevalent in Indian country side, arising out of financial paucity and largely due to lack of education and exposure to alternates available.

Arrangements were drawn up and food made ready for the old lady and the girls. They were not to go for collection of fire wood that day and were strictly warned not to wander far from the house. Narain drove away with the couple after giving each girl a paternal pat on the back.

"We shall be back before sunset and mind you do not leave the house" warned Saraswati, then turning towards Gauri she gently moved her palm on the girl's head and said,

"Do take care of your Grandmother and the girls dear", Gauri nodded in dutiful affirmation. All the girls cheered and waved at Narain as he drove away.

Shyamala in particular seemed very comfortable with the way Saraswati spoke of her family, daughters and the ailing mother-in-law and was keen to size up the girl for her Shankar. Krishnadas heard the proceedings silently and a little withdrawn.

"Our Shankar is a fine man with a very good notion of how to work a farm and keep the house. He has been a child to us from the day we found him near our lands. We are very sure if all goes well, your Gauri will find a good husband in him," goaded the lady further while her husband kept looking at the girl's father in silence. The couple have not even seen Shankar yet, he pondered unto himself. Just then Durgaprasad intervened.

"Narain here was mentioning that you will write off some lands to Shankar, we would very much like that to happen if every matter falls in line" pleaded the father wanting to secure his daughter's livelihood.

"We shall come along with Shankar to look up your daughter and if God wills and all goes well, we can look into these matters' said Krishnadas.

The date was fixed and after some more exchange of information the couple departed but not before Shyamala had fed them with hurriedly made simple fare for lunch, prior to betel nut chewing session woven around the subject of difficulties in cultivation, rising labour cost and ever depleting margins from farm produce.

Return was uneventful but for the stop at the town to pick up some savories to eat for the girls and a short meeting with Padma, Saraswati's domineering but intelligent sister-in-law. After briefing her, the couple requested the lady to come on the appointed day early.

"I will and will also get some things to spruce up our girl, "said Padma, happy at the prospect of helping out the girl, a victim of incestual rape and consequential trauma.

So it passed, on Wednesday, a week later, Krishnadas, Shyamala and Shankar were escorted to the household of Durgaprasad by the common friend.

Padma had come the previous evening and spent time explaining to a bewildered Gauri all that was to follow. It was perhaps more child-like curiosity in the girl and the desire to get away from the mundane life as well the ghastly memories of the past that she silently went through the ritual of dressing up with fineries to present herself to the prospective groom.

Shyamala drew the child to her lovingly and spoke first,

"Do you know how to cook, my child?", Gauri shook her head in affirmation and stole a glance at Shankar who must have been at least fifteen years her senior in age. He had already taken to the charming girl.

All three elders went and perched themselves under the tree where a mat had been laid out to talk the matter over and before long, there was general agreement. The ladies were engaged in small talk with Shyamala explaining to the mother and aunt the situation at their household, with a bit of exaggeration about Shankar's role and position in their household.

Durgaprasad had raised the matter of some land being written off to his daughter, to which he received no definite answer other than a nod from the land lord. After all, the entire expenditure of the marriage was being borne by the groom's party. It is not the custom in villages to ask the consent of the girl or her opinion in matters related to her own marriage. Some alliances are even fixed when the girl is a mere three to four years old. After all, Gauri was all of fourteen and had come of age, having attained puberty.

The marriage itself was a simple affair conducted late in the night or wee hours of the morning as indicated by the local astrologer, who having consulted the celestial positioning of stars, and declared that the couple would live in perennial bliss. Most relatives were present with whatever gifts possible. Saraswati had taken care that there would be no complaints about the food and Padma was ensuring that the grooms party was well taken care of.

Gauri left her birth place, her sisters, friends and parents that afternoon to a new life, new companions and a heart full of expectations of a decent life after the trauma that she had undergone at the hands of Surya who was conspicuously absent at the marriage.

It was past sunset that the party reached back to their village and after a brief welcome ritual and food, Gauri was led to the dwelling at the outhouse that was Shankar's living quarters, a single room with a make shift wash area. Shyamala had told Gauri that every morning she should come to the house and be with her doing the household chores.

"Come, Gauri, sit beside me", said Shankar and almost pulled her to his side, holding the wrist. There was a sharp sound of the glass bangle breaking and as the broken piece cut into her wrist, Gauri shrieked with pain and held her wrist tightly to stop the bleeding. Shankar stood up hurriedly to wet a cloth and wrapped it around the wrist, consoling his child wife and seated her on the bed. Pain had eased and Gauri wiped her face with the corner of her saree and looked at Shankar.

"I am very sleepy, can I take the pillow and lie down on the mat below?" she enquired of her husband almost pleadingly. The marriage, the timings, had taken its toll on the girl.

"You sleep beside me, today is our first night and you are talking of sleeping?"said Shankar. Gauri did not understand what he meant by that till he pinned her down on the bed and lifted her saree, looking lustily at her genitalia, Then got up, throwing aside his own Lungi* and soiled underwear, exposing an erection. Parting his young wives legs, Shankar unmindful of any foreplay and willingness of the girl entered her. Crouching on his knees he gave few powerful thrusts and with a groan ejaculated inside.

Almost immediately he withdrew and rolled back besides her and was snoring in a matter of minutes. Gauri was in slight pain and in shock at the suddenness of the entire happening. Her mind went back to the rabbit enclosure and could see in the eyes of her mind the Dove and the Buck. At that moment she wanted to inflict a sharp wound on Shankar just as the Dove had done, only in a totally different frame of mind. Such were the circumstances of Gauri's first night with her husband.

Gauri would spend the whole day from morning till dinner at the household of Krishnadas, cooking and cleaning the house while Shankar would tend to the work on the lands. Strange was the life for the girl having led a care free life at her parents place to have married and gotten into a back breaking life, only to be used as a sex object most nights. She would not even realize when Shankar would enter her and roll back to sleep and snore.

Indeed, Women are Chattels.

• Chapter 4 •

Flights of Fantasy

Many a night, Gauri would keep awake or even sit outside alone, legs stretched, aimlessly moving her palm over her lustrous hair. It was the first time she had seen motion pictures, serials and advertisement on the television in the afternoons when Shyamala would take a nap. She knew she was good to look at with those snake eyes and the perfectly shaped eye brows. By now she was aware of the constant stare she would get from men coming to meet the land lord or male labourers. She wanted nothing to do with any man but looked for that tenderness from Shankar which comes with a normal relationship. She had grown up listening to the stories of the virtues of Sita and Savitri from the Hindu mythology.

It is around this time, some six months into her married life that she started wanting to look and feel like those pretty damsels in the films and advertisements promoting perfumes, soaps, jewelry and the overnight fairness creams.

That night Shankar had come late in the night, staggering as usual after downing a couple of pegs of the local brew.

"What have you for me to eat?"

Gauri looked at her husband through her sleepy eyes, tired after the day's work,

"Nothing, we eat at the old man's house daily, don't we, you generally come when I am about to wind up the kitchen work. I always keep your dinner separately." She continued,

"Today you did not turn up and I thought you would eat somewhere and come." Replied the girl.

"Why did you not get my food here, you bitch," thundered Shankar, holding Gauri by her long thick hair, plaited neatly and pulled her inside the room, banging the door shut. The scared girl wanted to run away to the safety of the main house when he bolted the latch. All he wanted was to inflict pain on her.

Sitting down on the bed Shankar pulled out a bidi from the pack, held it tightly in between his yellowing teeth and lighted a match to it, puffing repeatedly. Taking out the smoking tobacco stick he looked intently at the glowing end and just then a faint smile appeared on his face, as if some amusing thought has passed his mind. Gauri stood by him holding a glass of water, still scared and apprehensive. Shankar took a deep gulp of the cool water, stood up and handing over the glass to his young wife, removed his sweat soiled shirt, threw it on the ground and motioned Gauri to get on the mat.

What followed left a deep scar in her mind, as well as on the left thigh of the girl.

Gauri knew what was to follow, she simply lifted her dress and waited for her husband to get into a squatting position, put all his weight on his feet, pull her thighs apart and enter her. Few hard thrusts, a grunt and a squirt, all would be over. Nothing like that happened, instead Shankar moved his palm softly over her smooth skin and genitals.

"Next time if I am late get my food here itself, Gauri, sometimes I do not want to face the old lady." Said Shankar, still looking intently and caressing the thighs.

"Why, do you have to go every evening with that milk vendor, you could be in the house and watch the television. Every day some nice film comes," prompted Gauri, waiting for a reaction, her legs still wide apart and Shankar still crouching and bending over her. Still moving his palm over the bulging crotch.

"Come early if you want after little drinks, not so much that you have had today and eat. They will not even notice".

"Just get my food here next time I am late and do not interfere with my routine, girl" said Shankar, little in irritation and mostly in stupor. Gauri resigned herself in submission as he pulled her a little closer holding her back and penetrated deep. There was some hardness in his facial contour that night as he gave some quick thrusts and lighted a cigarette his friend, the milk vendor had given while parting company.

Still moving back and forth now with more vigour, Shankar ejaculated with louder than usual grunt and jabbed the smouldering butt on the left thigh of the girl causing her to shriek out in pain. There seemed to be a smirk on Shankar's face as if the pain he had inflicted on his wife was sexually gratifying to him.

Kicking sharply, Gauri extricated herself and rubbed the burnt spot to shake off the charred skin. "What a monster you are", she shouted and ran out into the open still moaning in pain. Pouring water on the spot only increased the painful sensation initially. She just slumped down, leaning against the wall outside, tears rolling down her cheek uncontrollably.

That night Gauri, had slept leaning against the wall, unaware of the bright moon offering cool solace. The nights were pleasant with the monsoon about to set. Her mind focused on the nothingness of life's realities. Images of past, playground, little sisters, the darkness of the forest, flashing through her semi-conscious mind like fleeting glimpses of ghosts. Shankar slept through the night.

"Oh, you have come early today and looking a disaster, why?", Was the first reaction of Shymala, the next morning. The woman was used to Gauri reporting for work only by eight in the morning and not at the wee hour of six. The girl sat down to wash the soiled cooking vessels of the previous night looking sharply at Krishnadas who had just walked in for his cup of steaming coffee.

"How come you are early child?', he too questioned the girl, which again went unanswered, as Gauri continued scrubbing the blackened stains.

"Is all well child?", asked the man and this drew a sharp reaction as Gauri in a soft tone, almost inaudible said,

"Yes," and abruptly got up to wash the utensils in flowing water from the tap. The couple looked at each other and shrugged. They had, as time will tell, nothing much to lose. Any further probing would only bring problems to our doors is what Krishnadas had told his wife when the girl was busy tending to the calves downstairs.

That is when they heard the loud noise. Gauri was hitting the cow, the bald one with a stick, while the animal tried to protect itself by charging at the tormentor, the loving Gauri, it had known till last night. Perplexed, the aging couple rushed down only to join the farm hand who milked the cows as a daily chore, aghast at Gauri's presence and the outrage.

The stern, questioning look only got a mono toned reply from the girl.

"This one tried to gore me when I tried to caress it," said Gauri.

"But you are never required here, with the animals at this hour child, why are you here today instead of being with Amma?' asked the Patriarch visibly agitated.

There was a silence and what the girl said sealed her fate.

"I wanted to be with the animals as they are far better than humans, only this one", she said pointing at the cow, "wanted to hurt me". Throwing the stick, Gauri ran back to the house wiping her face on the sleeve of her blouse.

The generally cheerful girl was now a shadow of her past self. Mostly withdrawn and absent mindedly going through the chores in the landlord's house. Shankar was his usual self, unmindful of Gauri's agony,who was saddled with the past trauma and further compounded by his behavior. The elderly couple were perturbed at the turn of the events. They had gone through all this to ensure some semblance of settlement in the life of their charge, as well as, someone to manage the daily chores.

"Gauri stands in front of the mirror admiring herself constantly these days,' lamented the lady, looking at her husband.

"She has even started neglecting the work and I often see her standing and talking to the fellow who buys our coconuts". Krishnadas raised his head away from the newspaper and looked questioningly at his wife.

'What is the problem with that, Madan interacts with everyone on his visits to our lands whenever he comes to check the trees or pluck the bunches?", he asked.

Lady was silent for a while," That fellow has a way with women", she spoke in whispers. A hint of smirk on his face, and the old gent just took to reading his news.

Gauri had just then walked in. Her gait a bit sprightly and the neatly tied thick long black hair sporting a strewn up bunch of Jasmine flowers. Fresh and fragrant, adding that much more to her already radiant beautiful face. She swiftly disappeared in the kitchen. Shyamala gave a quick glance at her husband and left to join the girl in the kitchen. Man was lost in the news brief on sharing of the river waters between the two states bordering each other near the village. Any deviation from the stand taken by his own state would have a disastrous effect on the ground level of water. Agriculture contributed heavily to the state's GDP.

"You need not worry, Amma," answered the girl when questioned about her interaction with the wholesale purchaser of the coconuts. All the while cutting the vegetables for the afternoon meal. Gauri had not even lifted her head from the cutting board as if nothing mattered to her.

"Where did you get the Jasmines from, my girl?"

"Madan had got some for the women who work for him, he gave me one as well". Said Gauri, still not looking at the lady. How very defiant the girl has become, Shyamala thought, she had no clue of the sexual torments that the girl had gone through at a tender age and now at the hands of the very man she had, had her, tied with.

The self-admiration in front of the large mirror, use of powders and perfumes were on the rise. Gauri would sit and gaze at the colour pictures of those stars and starlets in the magazines lying around for hours together or just watch them intently on the TV Set. Her mind, seeing herself like the girl in an item number or the very charming personality of the heroin, walking hand in hand, in the park, cozying up to the film's hero. She had that coy smile about her these days, interrupted by the ugly nakedness of life whenever Shankar presented himself.

Sometimes Gauri herself would find the situation strange. It was as if she was drifting constantly from one body to the other. There was constant contradictions. She would visualize images of indulging in proactive sexual acts at times and the other prudish and inactive. Like a sprightly Doe or a log of wood. Like a blooming rose or a thorny stem. Never once she in her fantasy saw any known face. Fleetingly though Madan would exchange places with the Hero.

Much to her discomfort and anxiety, Shyamala, found the girl occasionally in intimate conversation with the Coconut buyer. Madan had not once kept the accounts in abeyance and it would be wrong to chastise the man. More over at times Krishnadas had taken cash in advance from him to tide over the financial difficulties. The worldly wise woman knew better.

Shankar was totally lost in his world dealing with the farm hands, and more so with his friend the milk vendor, probably unaware of the happenings around himself. Totally in a stupor. Gauri was for him nothing beyond an organism living for sexual satiation, not over three to four minutes. Now that too reduced to occasional copulation. Gauri could not stand his body odour,on the contrary, Madan was drenched in perfume. The Greek God.

The balcony of the house overlooked the entire lands and generally the couple would perch themselves there chatting and overlooking the activity while Shankar went about allotting the work and overseeing the workers. It served another purpose now a days. Gauri would often come over to the balcony, her eyes searching for Madan. Her face now very different, taken care of, with various toiletries and make up material gifted by the man. Shyamala had seen through all this and had ignored the happenings, anticipating problems in future.

"We shall be visiting Amma's sister in nearby town from Friday for a week", Krishnadas informed Shankar that evening over dinner.

"Is there any problem at their house?" asked the man knowing well the family issues surrounding Shyamala's family.

"No, nothing but her husband has not been keeping well, we want to go and look him up", said Krishnadas, "you will have to be extra careful and see that labour does not fool around."

"What about the cattle? You will have to sleep in the shed and keep an eye on them and the house", declared

Shyamala, looking at Gauri who was standing listening to the discussion.

Nodding at the directions given to him, Shankar got up finishing the last morsel and washed his hands while Gauri poured the water. That night the girl mostly kept awake oscillating between the Flights of fantasy.

• Chapter 5 •

Blow Hot Blow Cold

Shyamala went about getting the house cleaned by the girl and locking up most rooms and Krishnadas took stock of the work situation along with Shankar and chalked out the work flow for the week of their absence. Not that he needed to. All was known to the fellow.

"You sleep during the night in the cattle shed", Krishnaprasad instructed, adding further that Gauri should be in the main house after locking up the main door.

And so it came to pass, Krishnadas informed all who met him in the next two days, about the impending seven day trip, including Madan. Come Friday, the couple left for the town some seven hours away by the interstate bus service. That evening Shankar ate and motioned to his wife to lock up and come to the shed. There he lay down on the bed made for him, asking Gauri to press his limbs. Soon the man was snoring, tired after a day's grueling work. The girl went back to the house, ate a hurried meal and settled herself in the balcony.

Bright full moon was throwing its cool light over the orchard, Coconut and Gooseberry trees and the Paddy field. Night was silent except for the croaking of the frogs, noise of crickets and rustling of the leaves as soft wind blew through the large segmented leaves of coconut trees. Gauri wanted to wade through the winding pathways, soaking the moonlight, like the heroin in white clothes sailing with her beloved. Both drenched in the soft glow of the moonlight.

Just then her eyes focused on the small glowing light, diminishing in white screen of smoke and then glowing again. Someone was leaning against the tree and looking towards the house with a cigarette in his fingers. Gauri leaned forward to get a better look. The person was wearing white trousers and white shirt. She instantly felt in her bones the presence of Madan. A chill ran down her spine.

"What are you doing here at this time of the night?", questioned Gauri, having come down and tiptoed to the place where she had spotted Madan.

"I was here nearby to meet someone and could not contain myself from trying to see you. Last two days you have not been coming to the fields. I wondered what has happened to you", said Madan. "Where is Shankar?" he further probed looking all sides.

"He is sleeping in the cow shed".

There was complete silence for a while both looking deeply into each other's eyes.

"You do not know how much I look forward to spending some time with you in isolation, away from everyone" said Madan

"Why", asked the girl with a projected innocence and with a hidden smile on her face, only lips making slight moment.

Madan, a very seasoned person with all the requisite experience, knew at once that there was an invitation in the naughty innocence of the woman. This encouraged him to place his palm on her shoulder saying,

"You are looking so beautiful in the moonlit night. I want to hold you in embrace and keep kissing you on your ruby red lips".

Unknown to herself the very manifestation of her psyche was undergoing the change at that very moment and she slipped into Madan's arms lifting her face with lips protruding slightly open. Madan held hers in between his and sucked greedily, breathing heavily. Just then there was a noise of dried leaves getting ruffled. They quickly parted, alarmed, looking different ways for the cause.

This is a very common occurrence in farms as snakes or small creatures go looking for food and scurry around the lands in the night.

Madan hurriedly told her to meet him during the day.

"I will tell you what to do tomorrow," he said, holding her hands momentarily and passing her a tube of face cream. Nothing untoward happened that night.

Gauri was very attentive towards Shankar the morning after the happening under the tree. Perhaps there was a slight guilt and psychic oscillation once again.

"Amma and Anna not there, what shall I make for you for lunch"?, she asked, while Shankar feasted on the roti's and egg curry she had made.

"I don't know, make what you want", said Shankar continuing,

"I may go away with Govind to the cattle sale shandy. He wants to get a cow for himself after lunch".

"Will you be returning late and eat your dinner?" Gauri questioned out of genuine concern.

He simply nodded and left for the fields. Leaving a very confused wife behind.

Locking the house up after generally cleaning up, she went down to while away her time at the cattle shed. The farm hand came with a large bundle of green fodder and spread the same in front of the cows and some tender ones for the calf

"Why don't you come to the fields and see how the flowers are blooming on the gooseberry trees?" he said, adding that all farm hands and Shankar were very busy applying manure to the trees for a bountiful harvest.

"What else is going on, I will come after preparing lunch"

"Nothing much, Madan Sir is also applying complex to the roots of the Coconut trees, so he is there with his bunch of workers, all women with the gang leader Savitri". He said and walked away, leaving Gauri in contemplative mood. She stood at the water trough for the cattle for a while looking at her reflection in the still waters. There was a loose strand of hair which she carefully tucked behind her ear and moved her palm over the hair to smoothen the unevenness.

She was contemplating what to make for lunch, simple but satiating for Shankar. Never was she able to grasp as to why her mind and body craved for anything else or moves between two different levels of psychic imbalance. She knew Shankar liked the Dal cooked with Drumsticks and rice. Plucking a few near the house she went about doing just that.

Madan had seen Shankar pillion riding and going away that too with the milk vendor on his two wheeler. He knew the Bandicoot will only return late at night inebriated.

"I am going to the other orchard, you get the work done here properly, without anyone whiling away the time" Madan warned the person in-charge, looked around and drove away on his Royal Enfield. It was nearing noon and soon would be time for lunch. Generally the labour would take time off to eat and rest for a while. Today the schedule got shifted.

Madan, in the meanwhile, rode the bike taking a circuitous route to the gap in the Aloe Vera fencing at the back of the house and entered with the engine silenced, parking behind the growth of mushrooming Banana plants.

The door was not locked and he stealthily moved in to find Gauri lying on a mat, her hand resting on her eyes. Madan's gaze was fixed on the slowly rising and lowering of the perfectly shaped chest in harmony. He stood in total silence with bated breath contemplating his move. Time seemed to melt ever so gradually. His own breath warming up and his heart beats increasing in counts.

It was a few minutes before Madan mustered strength enough to go noiselessly and position himself besides her on his knees. Gauri might have sensed something in her slumber to suddenly remove her hand from the eyes and look at the intruder. She sat up with a jerk.

"No, no, Gauri please keep calm and lie down", said Madan and placed his broad palm on her thighs.

"How did you get in?" were the only words she could speak out, while Madan encircled her back with the other hand.

"Door was open and I came in without anyone becoming wiser", he whispered. "You were looking so enchanting and unaware of the world around you", Madan paused looking deep into those captivating eyes, and continued.

"Specially me, suffering with the desire to engulf you in my arms". His nectar laced words slowly sinking in and taking effect over the mind of the dazed girl.

Gauri was unaware of her own condition. Most times she would unknowingly feel mesmerized and fragmented, oscillating between the reality and the make believe.

Madan held her in tight embrace and feverishly started kissing her on the lips and face. Being adept at the art of making love, he was aware of the erogenous parts of female body that would when lightly touched with finger tips or the warm caress of the lips, bring out sexuality in women.

He was then moving his lips slowly and purposefully between her jaw and the shoulder and could sense her body heat rising. Slowly Madan loosened his hold and gently pushed on her back in a supine position, while continuing to arouse her with his lips and fingers. Sliding down a little he started planting passionate kisses on her bare stomach in between the blouse and the saree. Gauri had never experienced anything like this before and there was a strange wetness in between her thighs.

Madan lifted his head and stared at her with a gentle smile. There was a glow on the face, sort of a redness that comes with the rise of adrenalin.

"Lock the door", said Gauri now almost pleadingly. There was a constriction in her pelvic region.

Back at her, Madan now emboldened, had placed his palm encircling her bared well rounded chest in his large palm. Slightly squeezing it, while with the other he caressed her left cheek, deftly moving them occasionally on her half open lips feeling the heat of her exhalation.

His right palm had now moved on her leg and was tugging at the hindrance of the saree, trying to reach the bareness of her thigh.

Unknown to herself and keeping in with the natural sequence of exploding nerves, she parted her thighs.

Madan was burning. His heart beats, racing and making the fast rhythmic beat like the Royal Enfield, reached for her lips and they both kissed feverishly for a few minutes.

Gauri by now was almost reciprocating in a rhythmic movement and then with a hoarse almost muted cry, burst into ecstasy that comes with a full orgasm. She was in a stance, never having experienced the pleasure other than a pain full, piercing thrust, leaving her bitter and at times lacerated.

Madan with a pleasing smile held her face with both the palms, looking deep into her snake eyes,

The Sun had advanced in the west throwing an orangish yellow glow through the open large window facing the balcony, pleasantly warming up the room. The air inside was already filled with the mild scent of Jasmine that had fallen loose from Gauri's hair. The perfume of the Sandal Wood scent from Madan, intermingling with this, doused the already over charged sensuality and they both lay in perfect union for a while, without any movement, devouring each other.

Gauri burst into orgasm with a shriek and a copious wetness. Both in tight embrace meshed as if a single individual.

"Please don't stop", pleaded Gauri, now having lost the initial shyness now wanting more of her lover. Her body, burning with the mixed emotions of extreme desire and gratitude. Picking the edge of her saree, she patted dry the perspiration off Madan's forehead.

Then the obvious happened as Madan with heavy breathing, perspiring and with a final grunt like a thundering stallion, poured all of himself inside Gauri who reciprocated for the fifth time.

The heat of the west ward Sun had mellowed as the lovers seem to melt into each other. They lay holding each other for a while and shortly Madan stood up tidying himself. Gauri too, in the meanwhile rearranged her garments and the long luxurious hair. They exchanged a smile. Not a word was spoken.

Madan bent down, planting a kiss on her cheek and pushed some money in her palm.

"Please get yourself whatever dress you desire next you go to market", He said," "I shall get you some perfume, powder etc. soon". Madan departed the way he had come, leaving behind a very exhausted and confused girl. She did not want the money. She never had any.

Tucking the cash inside her blouse, Gauri went down to the cattle shed. The cows were sitting and chewing the cud. Occasionally twirling the tail to chase away the stray fly. She sat on a bundle of green fodder, resting her arm on large stone next to it. The Sun was milder and the rays pleasingly warm. Soon she dozed off, her body wearing off the sexual exhaustion.

Fleeting clouded images were passing through her almost unconscious mind. Men dressed in total black with a whip in their hand hitting out at some figure tied up like the white cow, struggling to free herself. Then there would be a total reversal in images with herself running with open arms dressed in fineries among flower patches towards the rising moon in full bloom, throwing white cool rays amidst rows of coconut trees. Then again the figure in agony and some stranger in black shouting at her to get up.

The voice resounding in her stupor might have been the thundering command of Shankar totally inebriated, swaying both ways. Sometimes front and back, sometimes sideways. The first thing Gauri sensed was the stench from his body odour and the smell of strong country liquor, as she got up with a jerk. He was standing, his hand firmly resting on her shoulder.

"What are you sleeping here for at this hour, you slut," shouted Shankar, pulling her by the shoulder. Gauri was defiant not wanting to get near her husband and out of sheer abhorrence shouted back.

"What do you want me to do, I was tired and simply dozed off while you went away to drown yourself in liquor", she said, not even looking at him. This, while the milk vendor, was present at the scene, witnessing the ugliness of Shankar's uncouth and sadistic character.

"You bitch, how dare you talk this way to me", shouted the man with a high pitched thunderous shout, shaking the frightened Gauri violently and planting a sharp slap on her cheek. She staggered and tried to balance herself but fell down and out fell the neatly folded money from her blouse. It was the milk vendor who pointed at the money and drew Shankar's attention to it.

"Where did you get the money from, you whore?" demanded Shankar, lifting the sobbing girl, with a swollen cheek. He was holding her by that luxurious hair she was known for and was proud of. Screaming in pain she offered the explanation in between convulsive sobs,

"I found it inside the house in a kitchen utensil," lied the girl. "Why are you behaving like this with me?, What wrong have I done to you?, pleaded Gauri, now looking straight in his eyes, perhaps to cover her own guilt of having spent that torrid afternoon with her lover. Shankar simply pocketed the cash and left for his own room calling her a thief and a crook having stolen the cash from his benefactors. Cows milked and with a smirk on his face the vendor left with the can.

"She deserves it", is all he told the attenders with a smile. Rejection at Gauri's hands of his own advances towards her was finally avenged thought the renegade.

That night she remained in the main house and Shankar kept to himself, deep in sleep in the room. Gauri tossed around unable to sleep. Some weirdness in her behavior. She was not even thinking of the pain inflicted on her, nor was she thinking of Madan. She was in a totally different dimension of mental variations that were taking a grip on her mind. She was up and making up her face with available creams and powder in the house. Carefully removing the red vermillion from her hair parting, a mark of a married woman and placing a large round red circle on her forehead. She looked mesmerizing by any standards.

Gauri continued looking at herself in the mirror. Admiring her own beauty, unmindful of the stinging pain around her cheek. She unknown to herself was transforming.

Gauri had manifested as Maya and was running towards the bright moon, open armed, In all the fineries and the jewelry. She heard someone calling her.

"Maya, Maya, come to me", said the voice and she responded spontaneously turning, all the while with a broad smile towards the swaying coconut trees where the voice was coming from.

"Ah, there you are, I waited for so long for this moment. The moon light guided me to this grove you told me to come." Maya was breathing heavily when he put his arm around her waist pulling her closer. Hand in hand they walked the path towards the flower patch to sit down on the bench. This was a sublime moment, She was resting her head on his broad shoulders. He was caressing her hair and telling her all that he did that day in minute details. Maya was listening in complete awe of her hero, nodding sometimes and responding with an yes in affirmation at times. There was complete love and trust between them. She could lean on him forever.

She continued to rest her head against the tree trunk, deep in slumber while the soothing rays of moon caressed her with the wind blowing cold.

• **Chapter 6** •

The Drift

Gauri was up early the next morning and after a quick wash got down to cooking rice and the curry to go with it. She knew that Shankar would soon be around for that steaming mug of coffee and then settle down to eat before making for the fields.

Only she wondered how she found herself against tree in the flower patch all alone dressed and made up well devoid of the vermillion from the parting of the hair. She was relieved though that no one had seen her that night.

Like clockwork, the life went on for the next couple of days. Krishnadas and Shyamala had come back too from their short sojourn. Shyamala was the one to notice the unusual and altering behavior in the girl.

"Gauri looks possessed and at times in deep depression", she told Krishnadas,

"I have seen her sitting vacant eyed looking into oblivion", adding further details," You know I am afraid she may burn down the kitchen and herself if she does not mind and tend to the fire". Shyamala was waiting for the reaction from her husband.

"She is often complaining of headache too", she continued and there was a bit of irritation evident in her contour, not getting any response from her husband. Sensing this Krishnadas spoke in a hushed voice.

"May be she is pregnant Shyamala, or maybe you are making a mountain out of an ant hill'.

"Neither, I know something is amiss and there is hardly any interaction between the girl and Shankar. She just sits in a trance hardly moving a limb at times and mind you, her fetish about making up is also taking a dangerous turn." She said

"How so", now the old man seemed interested.

"She is so pretty with excellent features and Shankar", Shyamala's face showing disgust now went on, "Is so unkempt and shoddy. Why does she give so much importance to her looks?". She paused and commented, "No there is more to it than meets the eye". Such was the finality in her talk that nothing but silence followed for some time, both contemplating, in their minds, associating this, with Madan and unable to figure out the disassociation.

There was not much happening around the lands this time of the year with almost most of the pre monsoon preparation having been done. If any, one could see the heavenly activity building up in the skies with greyish black clouds hovering to perform the monsoon dance that bring respite and new lease of life for trees and plants.

Gauri spent most of her free time with the cattle, hardly ever talking to others or watching channels showing films portraying romance and intrigues of life.

Many a times her mind would drift in the past, particularly painful reflections were the ones she suffered in childhood in the forest. She was not able to forgive Surya. The life with and the treatment by Shankar did not seem to matter to her. She was in a way resigned to fate.

One of the pregnant cows was about to deliver and it was showing all signs of discomfort and labour. Almost all the farm hands were around. Gauri was watching the proceedings with keen interest. The animal was sitting and then getting up, spreading the hind as if in expectation. Pain written large on the face. Once in a while it would bellow and try to look behind.

The vaginal passage had broadened and the cow was now straining, trying to eject her offspring. Some fluid would ooze out, strained with blood red streaks. Gauri was watching with keen interest and unknown to herself moved closer to Amma. The streaks of blood and mucus was revolting and Gauri was about to throw up, when it happened. Very slowly the hoof appeared, bagged in the placenta. Expectation was high in the onlookers. Then the bundled up head of the calf, totally resting on the little legs, eyes closed. The mother strained further, her hind legs wide apart.

It took a while but out fell the calf, very smoothly, draped in the transparent membrane. There was a gush of uterine fluid, mostly red. Gauri swooned and fell down and again the transformation took place.

Then came the dream, Maya was fond of sparkling white clothes and looked charming in the chiffon sari and blouse. Her deep neckline showing the cleavage and the enormity of her well rounded breasts. Her nose ring studded with diamond sparkling in the bright sunlight of the day. There was complete solitude and silent rustle of wind through the bushy flowering plants. The wind had a fragrance as it whispered through the Champa* trees.

Suddenly he came from behind her, encircling the waist, placing his clean shaven face next to hers.

"Darling, you are exuding charm", he said, turning her towards him. He was a tall handsome man with sharply shaped moustaches to match his well-groomed hair.

"Where are you taking me today"?, Maya asked him tenderly stroking his chest.

"You always wanted to go on a river cruise, Maya, I have arranged for us to take a sailing boat and go down stream. The river is not in full spate as of now. We can have a slow, smooth sail". Nothing was more agreeable to Maya. What would be better but the romantic company of her prince charming, that too down a river?

It was early in the evening as they rode in his white Safari to the river bank. Holding the hand, he guided her to the sailing boat and motioned to the oarsman to proceed. The boat slid into the waters as the man gave a push with the large oar, as Maya slumped on the bench. He held on to her and then positioned himself next to her.

The breeze was gently cool and the moon just on the rise with a soft glow of whitish orange tint. The setting was perfect and replicated closely the cellulous effect of the screen.

The sail was up, off white with dirt and competed for Maya's attention when he gently pulled her close resting her head on his shoulder. She sighed, sliding her arm to hold his back. The blissful moments melted away in time as the boat drifted further into the depths of the water. None was aware of the time that has passed by.

Sometimes a tributary joining the river can cause the whirlpool effect and this was causing the boat to rock. Maya swayed from left to right holding tightly on to him almost digging her nails into the flesh of her paramour.

"Gauri, take hold of yourself", was what Amma was screaming as the girl dug into the flesh of the old lady's arm, slightly shivering but now coming to her senses. Seething in anger because of the pain Shyamala stood up, her husband behind her. Both were aghast at the suddenness of the situation.

"Demons have possessed this girl", proclaimed Shyamala, rubbing her skin vigourously to do away the pain. Gauri had sat up in a daze. She had no connect with physical happening just a short while back with the cattle. There was no connect at all, Period.

That night Shankar, drunk and smelly as always, slept in a noisy stupor without a care for the young wife.

Little after the dawn, the small transport vehicle had driven in with ladders, ropes, sickles and men. Harvest day for coconuts. Shortly after them, the Royal Enfield sounding it's rhythmic beat carried Madan in. Work was tedious but rewards good. Around ten that morning almost half the plucking of tender nuts was done with when the workers sat down to eat the heavy breakfast arranged by the contractor. Madan looked at the smiling girl in amusement.

"Amma has sent me to fetch few nuts" Gauri told the man almost avoiding his steady mirthful gaze.

"Take as many you want and for yourself too', he said pointing at the large mound of nuts heaped in the shade.

"Please ask one of your men to take them to the house, about ten of them, she said now looking at Madan. Memories of the encounter with him, bringing a flush on her radiant face.

"Let them finish with eating, I will arrange so", he motioned to her to sit while he stood leaning against a Palm of coconut little away from where the workers were squatting.

There was silence except for the rustling of the large serrated leaves swaying in the mild breeze. Madan looked upwards,

"Gauri, I know all about the ill treatment meted out to you by Shankar". He said still looking up as if not to meet the eyes of the woman. "and that no good fellow Gopal has him under his thumb. Be wary he has his eyes set on you, my dear".

Most times sympathy from even a distantly known person can have deep rooted effect on a person and this is exactly what Madan was trying to achieve. Unaware of the fact that his sexually sensuous encounter with Gauri has had far more impact than he could imagine. She was in total awe of him having experienced a painless and exotic experience first time in her life right through the childhood to adolescence.

"what am I to do?", she lamented, "I have been through hell all my life till now and I know that is my fate. I have resigned to it". Madan could see the deep anguish in the doe eyed one. This is the moment to cement my relationship with her is all the man could think of.

"Don't you bother Gauri, I am with you and matters will fall in place. I know you were deprived of the cash I gave you. Here take this and get a beautiful dress". Madan was visualizing her well rounded breast encircled in his palm, while he handed over some cash.

Both were unaware that Shankar stood glued to the ground staring at them from near the room, still with a hangover. The laborer was carrying the tender nuts to the house, still attached to the stack followed by a cheerful Gauri.

"What were doing with that son of a bitch, you slut", Shankar demanded to know, holding her by the long strand of hair. Gauri shrieked in pain, her eyes welling up and turning crimson.

"Leave me alone, I was sent to get the nuts for them. Then raising her voice she shouted,"why do you treat me so" and tugged hard at her hair pulling it loose from Shankar's grip. The impact of the pull and his own physical condition caused the man to tumble and fall, injuring his elbow in the process.

"You whore, if I ever find you talking to that man, I shall give you such a thrashing that you will regret the day you were born", shouted Shankar still fallen on the ground.

Gauri had already run away to join the boy with the nuts. She hardly spoke the whole day. Shankar too never came for lunch. The old couple kept to themselves. The girl too, had just nibbled at her food. She wondered at the emptiness of her life. The basic element of human happiness, the humble treasures of love, marriage, home and family. The deprivation that Gauri felt for the familial warmth and stability was simply overwhelming.

It was as if she was an infantile and divided personality, her own self peeling away from the usual identity of hers, manifesting itself into a distinctly different identity.

That dreadful night after winding up with the household chores early, Gauri lay down in the room. The mental fatigue, almost overpowering her senses.

"He should be here in a while now", Maya was talking to herself. She had woken up from a shallow slumber to do herself up. The mirror reflected the sheen on her well defined, beautiful face. She loosened the strands of her hair and began to stroke it with steady long downward movement of the brush. She stepped out to gaze at the path way lit by the bright moon looking eagerly for her man.

The images of lovely moments spent in the arms of her lover swept past her mind as a lovely and sensuous dream. She could feel the goose pimples arise all over her body. Back at the mirror she looked at herself smilingly in known anticipation and dabbed her lips with moisturizer bringing out the pinkish glow to her already ruby red, petal like lips. She was ready to receive him engulfing his fullness in it's entirety emotionally and physically. The wetness was soaking itself into the inner garment.

Maya sat legs stretched out in the glow of the moon waiting for him, to behold him and to be beheld in his gaze, looking into her eyes, his palm caressing her cheeks and accidentally slipping down to her thin waist and below. The cool breeze and the whitish glow of the moon seemed to caress her whole body and she slowly slipped into drowsiness.

Suddenly she was aware of the presence of an intruder. Maya wanted to get up but was pinned down by the foul smelling man, his strong arms and large palms at her knee pulling the legs apart at the same time.

"Oh my God, leave me alone, please", begged Maya, as the stranger started pulling her saree upwards, trying to position himself between her thighs.

"No, no, please I beg you do not force yourself on me like this, I belong to someone else." Maya screamed while trying to push the intruder away with both her hands. Her strength equaling the agonizing trauma that she was experiencing at that very moment.

The intoxicated intruder fell back unable to keep his balance.

"You slut, how dare you treat me this way", he shouted behind the disheveled damsel in distress. Maya, as if in a frenzy was rushing in while the man staggered and stood up. Her effort at closing the door was in vain as the man banged against the closing door with all his weight. Everything was happening at lightning speed and all it took was a little over a few seconds for Maya to snatch the sickle lying on the platform.

She dashed at the intruder and brandishing the tool at the menacingly advancing man, waved it in air. The recently sharpened farmer's tool found it's mark leaving a deep cut in the left shoulder and neck.

Bleeding copiously Shankar staggered out in pain, now out of the stupor he was in, to save himself from further punishment.

Maya slumped down, utterly exhausted, confused and fearful at the sudden turn of events. Her usually radiant face covered in perspiration. The vermillion from the forehead sliding down her eyes and cheek in a strange pattern mixed with her sweat.

What followed was a period of long silence except the barking of stray dogs that had made the farm their home.

Time had stopped that night.

All hell broke at six in the morning when the men came for milking the cattle. Shankar was lying down in semi – comatose state with small a pool of coagulated blood that had oozed from his shoulder and there was some dried crimson red patch on the neck where the sickle had left a gash.

"What has happened to Shankar? Is he dead?"the old man was enquiring leaning on his protégé and shaking him up. Now Shyamala had also come down and seeing Shankar in such a state, let out a loud shriek in horror.

"Gauri, Gauri, she shouted and ran towards the dwelling. She found the door open and the girl still in deep slumber.

"Get up and come fast, see what has happened to our Shankar, how could you be sleeping girl and why is your face covered with vermillion"?, Shyamala kept shouting insistently, only stopping when she saw the blood stained sickle by the girl.

"What have you done, have you killed your own husband"?, she shouted now looking into the bewildered eyes. Shyamala had now traced her steps back to the door more in fear and giving a look back at Gauri, ran towards the cattle shed where Krishnadas was bent over Shankar with a jug of water trying to revive him. Gopal, the milk man, was there too when all eyes turned to the girl who was running towards them screaming.

"What has happened to him?" screamed Gauri, now bending over Shankar who was just opening his eyes.

The blood, the disheveled girl, the onlookers and the very suspicious old couple all presented a very gory sight. A perfect setting for things to come.

"What have you done to Shankar, tell me woman, I have seen enough to know that you have tried to kill him", shouted Shyamala, loosing all self-control and accusing a very disturbed Gauri.

"Amma I did not do anything and I do not know how my husband is lying here in a pool of blood. Please get him to the doctor first". She pleaded almost in tears looking at a very anxious Krishnadas.

None believed her, but nevertheless, Shankar was taken for treatment where he narrated the happenings of the night once he regained most of his senses.

The obvious happened in Gauri's life. Narain was called and after some altercations, she was sent packing back to her parents house.

Gauri remained unaware of what had transpired. She for one was the last to swat at the fly even if it bothered her, constantly buzzing around the eyes.

Life for her was nothing but a drift now.

• Chapter 7 •

Agony and the Ecstasy

DurgaPrasad more so, was a broken man, aged, overworked and now worried for his lovely child, who he earnestly believed was victim of circumstances. He for one, was not aware of the trauma, Gauri had gone through in her teens. Neither did Saraswati, was in the know.

Tongues would wag though in the village clusters.

"This bewitching woman would have spread her thighs for someone", was an open submission by most and that halted Gauri from socializing. Even her childhood friends kept away, much to her discomfort and anguish. The tree in the compound reminded her of Surya molesting her and the forest she shunned.

Gauri had narrated all that she had gone through to her Aunt Padma who was the only confidante who would understand her agony. All efforts by DurgaPrasad and Narain his friend, had failed to bring about the reconciliation.

Life still had to take the unexpected twists and turns in Gauri's life.

Padma while chatting with her husband brought out the girl's subject one evening after dinner. Their own children busy in their own world.

"Gauri has suffered much at the hands of fate. She does not deserve to go through so much mental and physical pain". Prakash nodded in agreement understanding his niece's condition and also in appreciation of his wife's concern.

"She is very harmless and is endowed with a helping nature. God knows what will become of her". He added.

"You know what worries me, is once a woman becomes friendless and just drifts, she can be the cause of inciting all sorts of desires including crime in others, especially men".

Husband understood enough to know that Padma was speaking the truth.

"You are right Padma, such a situation can make the girl helpless and migratory like a stray chicken in the world of foxes" said Prakash, looking at the domestic birds feeding on the street where some grain was scattered. Both were silent for a while. Lost in thought.

Soon enough, prodded by his wife and of his own desire to find some secure occupation for Gauri, the couple decided to find her a placement in the small town and shifted her to their home. The girl too was happy enough to leave behind the area that caused her to often shift into agonizing mood changes.

One advantage that Gauri had was her beautiful face, almost chiseled to perfection and a pleasant perpetual smile on the face, dotted with those captivating eyes.

Arranged by a common friend, Gauri now started working at a medium sized bakery owned by the local Brahmin gentleman. Sridhar Sharma hailed from a family of educated gentlemen deft in the craft of culinary art and education. His bakery would supply, on a daily basis, buns and breads to whole seller based in a larger township not far away and as well engage in the retail trade from the baking center itself. Sridhar's wife was a teacher in the only English medium school in the town. Initially Gauri was to manage the sales counter.

Sales picked up gradually, perhaps from the aroma emanating out of the freshly baked products and the added presence of the demure damsel. Sridhar was pleased and except from finding himself aroused at times found, Gauri occasionally lost as if in a trance, only to be rudely shaken by the irritated customer. Time passed. A known intimacy developed and the tongues wagged too.

Shabbir, the whole seller from the town was at the bakery and Sridhar met him with all warmth.

"I have come to see you today as the consignment you are sending to me daily is short in supply", complained the elderly gent stroking his peppered beard.

"We are very particular about not only you but all the supplies we make. This cannot be happening", protested Sridhar, not wanting to upset his best customer.

"Look, I know you well enough to understand there could be some other problem, but that can be easily addressed. Why don't you send someone in the bus along with the boxes? That way every transaction of goods as well the cash will be safe", suggested Shabbir Bhai.

"I for one, do not trust the bus staff, be it the cleaner, conductor or the driver of this service that you use".

Sridhar pondered over the issue, while the Muslim gentleman sipped the tea from the small glass container.

"Can you suggest some other service?"

"No Sridhar, we have been using this for a long time, better you arrange for someone to accompany the boxes and I shall pay one way charges while you do the other". He said in a firm tone.

This settled, Gauri was taken off the counter to carry forward the wishes of Shabbir Bhai. She would accompany the consignment, collect the cash and return way before evening fell.

The turn of events in her life is what caused the biggest damage, unknown to her.

The private buses carry packages and passengers to small inter-state towns in India, charging for both. These vehicles are equipped with seat on the other side of the driver and the imposing engine. More leg space gives the passenger a sense of physical comfort. Gauri, as a regular, was given the priority by the driver much to the annoyance of the conductor and the cleaner. These two anyway were annoyed at being deprived of the few packages they used to palm off.

Naushad, though much older than Gauri, looked like a Greek God with trimmed mustaches, broad shoulders and pleasant face to go with. Tall, handsome and easy with words and a roving eyes. Wife Tabassum had passed away two years back while in labour along with the still born.

A cordial and casual relationship between the driver and Gauri soon turned into mutual admiration. The new found experience of daily bus travel through pleasant country side and the companionship kindled in her a strong emotion as never experienced before. She had found a friend who she felt she could open up to and share all her worldly woes with. A very cherished experience, any one could have, for someone who has undergone physical and mental torture at an early childhood stage. Naushad, the crusader as his colleagues called him, knew that sympathy and some attention would further the relationship.

"Take some time off for yourself and do something enjoyable sometimes, Gauri".

He whispered to her when the bus had to be stopped for that hurried tea break, a time when passengers also relieved themselves.

She just laughed, half suppressing her bemusement at the suggestion.

"Where can I go all on my own", she said. He remained silent for a while, looking into her questioning eyes and said,

"You know I get four days off after every week of this arduous driving, maybe we can do things together." he said hurriedly,

"See a good cinema and eat something somewhere?.

Gauri said nothing, it was time to resume the journey.

Couple of days followed in intimate conversations and soon Gauri was contemplating informing Shridhar Sharma about her absence from work that Friday when Naushad would be on leave.

Capitol, the cinema hall was at the very vicinity of the small railway station in the town of Rangpur, adjoining the high way where Naushad lived. Gauri got down on the return trip after the delivery of the consignment. Naushad had two tickets for the show.

The plot was an absorbing story of two lovers constantly seeking each other's company surrounded in myriad of problems and social issues. Songs were so melodious and Gauri sat through the three hours her palm entwined in the large, strong palm of her companion. Occasionally wiping it on her saree, to rid the perspiration off, arising from the rising adrenaline.

That night she reached the bakery late in the evening to the annoyance of Shridhar Sharma.

"Here, please take the accounts", she said handing over the cash to him.

"Where did you go today for so long", Shridhar questioned her chidingly.

"Oh, just spent some time with a girl from the village", she said avoiding his eyes.

"Just see to it that you do not do this more often", he said with a sternness laced with some mistrust.

Agony follows ecstasy often.

• Chapter 8 •

The Pitfall

Winter was setting in and evenings seemed a bit longer. There was a gentleness about the cool breeze that waded through the small towns and country side. Life was just about floating through smoothly for everyone but Naushad.

His mind was constantly occupied with images and thoughts of the girl. He would see himself in her company in varied postures while driving or otherwise. The thought of possessing her was ruining his self and that reflected in his driving skills as well the general behavior. Such was the effect of the girl on men.

It did not take long for Naushad to try and turn the agony into ecstasy.

"Gauri, I want to marry you and settle down to a life of happiness. You have been deprived of it too". He pleaded while holding her hand some six weeks from the day they had gone to the cinema.

The meaning his words carried for Gauri was evident on her radiant face but it was devoid of any expression. They were seated beneath the imposing water tank near the small colony where Naushad had his rooms. There was never enough time or space for anything else.

"Will you keep me happy at all times and not desert me", enquired a wide eyed girl, amazed, doubt full and confused at the turn of events. She had grown to want her Greek God too.

"Never, only you will have to change your religion and Maulavi Saheb will give you a different name", Naushad, waited for her reaction.

Her nod opened up the skies that evening and there was a drizzle prompting them to hurriedly move to the bus stand for the girl to catch the bus back to the bakery. On the way back in the bus, Gauri was deep in a trance and in apprehension of the way life was taking a turn for her. Her desire for Naushad was strong enough to ward off any misgivings. Innocence is often the virtue that shelters the catastrophe unknowingly.

"Again you have taken off, inspite of my warning you last time that your periodic absence is going to cost you and me dearly Gauri", shouted a much agitated Shridhar Sharma, looking at the clock showing nine pm. She too stole a look at the moving hand of the large clock in the bakery and handed over the day's collection.

"Come on girl, speak up, what are you up to these days? Don't think I am not in know of your meetings with that driver friend of your's", shouted the bakery owner, pulling the girl inside the very baking room and slamming it shut.

Gauri's answer was calm and like a slap on his face.

"Sir, I have done nothing that amounts to cheating you or has any concern or consequence to you or your business. You have given me shelter when I needed it the most, I am thankful for that but I need some time off for myself too".

Shridhar could sense that the girl was highly agitated and in a state of extreme fatigue. A customer asked for a loaf of bread just then pulling curtains on any further altercations.

The bakery closed late that night. Shridhar persuaded Gauri to sleep in his house that night. This was not the first time, generally happened if work went on late in the night.

Padma and Prakash were in the know of this and anyway the teacher madam, Shridhar's wife was always there.

"Take these fruits and mat and just go up to the roof top and get some sleep".

"Where is madam? Has she gone to sleep", asked Gauri looking around a little apprehension evident on her face.

"She has gone to her parent's house just this evening", said the man and prepared to retire.

Gauri went up to the roof, spread the mat. The moon was peeping through the clouds and there was this pleasant cool breeze that swept through her luxurious black hair. The enchanting atmosphere and the smell of Naushad's attar from her palm peeled her away gradually from her own self. Time melted away into the unknown depths of mystery. Again the disassociation started.

"Maya, there you are", said he drawing her closer to his own self, strong attar made of roses penetrating her nostrils. She took a deep breath, smiled pleasantly at him, moving her palm on his face feeling the bristles of his neatly trimmed moustaches. Her fingers moved over the lips of her paramour.

"I have been waiting for you for so long", he said slowly making her sit next to him, all the while his strong arms encircling her tender slim waist. She now could feel his hand move over her bare stomach slowly moving towards her naval.

"Oh my God", she exclaimed as the sensation passed through her body. She could sense the hardening of her nipples.

She could barely comprehend what he was saying. Her own senses aroused so much that voluntarily she lay on her back, awaiting his next move.

"Oh Maya!, when would we become one body, one soul", she heard him murmur in trembling voice.

What is wrong with him wondered Maya, why does he take so long? All the while, slowly moving up and down, in a pulsating movement, of her pelvic zone.

Then it happened all of a sudden.

Maya felt the hand of a stranger firmly clasping her chest. All hell broke loose. She could never stand any other man touching her, that too today in his presence.

"Who are you and what are you doing here, how dare you touch me"? screamed the damsel in distress, holding on to the railing of the roof. Her clothes disheveled and hair in disarray.

"Gauri take hold of yourself, it is me Shridhar",whispered the bakery owner, lest the high pitched voice would bring the neighbours out.

She was still screaming and he continued shaking her. Finally to gain control over her, Shridhar slapped her hard as the lights were being turned on in the vicinities.

With almost a thud she sat down, dazed and hurting. Maya peeling away slowly.

Shridhar, sensing that there was something amiss and that the girl was not in total control of herself.

Inevitable happened. Gauri had to stop working as it was made abundantly clear by Shridhar's wife that the girl should have nothing to do with them. Account were settled.

If anyone, it was Naushad now who was preparing for the coup.

• Chapter 9 •

The Prognasis

Shridhar Sharma had all the reasons to be disturbed or baffled. It was the first time ever, he had experienced the sudden surge in his sexual urge and then to be faced with the dilemma of sneers from the spouse and acquaintances.

Morning walk group consisted of the influential locals. Dr. Gangadhar being one of them. MD, with a substantial practice. His wife, herself a post graduate, in medicine was the District Medical Officer. Doctor would often be seen in the company of many discussing local issues and taking keen interest in politics. After all the political party he supported had suggested that he may be given the seat for the next state elections. Becoming the state minister for health was something the medical man cherished.

That morning, Shridhar finding him alone, said,

"Sir, I would like to have your time exclusively to discuss a problem weighing down heavily on my mind. Can you spare some time away from the clinic?"

"Sure, let us meet at eight at the clinic and we can drive down to the open air bar at the far end towards the adjoining town", suggested the doctor. So was fixed. After all, Shridhar Sharma was an active member of the party.

That evening at the bar with their drinks, Shridhar narrated the whole incidence of Gauri and his own vows.

After having drowned two drinks doctor was more forth right with his comments.

"Look Sharma, I happen to know something about this girl's background from past. She may be suffering with Dissociative Identity Disorder or also known as Multiple Personality Disorder". Doctor waited for his words to sink in. Shridhar looked shockingly blank and intently at him.

"This disorder usually starts in childhood. It is three to nine times more prevalent in females than in males. This generally is caused by sexual abuse and violence in childhood. This problem is taking serious proportions in our country and has to be dealt with the seriousness it deserves. The rape of any kind has a magnitude much higher than assumed by us, in leaving a girl child shattered for life". The doctor's words were now taking deep effect on the listener.

"Sir, but I experienced some very strange behavior in the whole personality of this girl that night. It was as if she was a totally different person. I even heard her shout and call some fellow pleading him to come and save his Maya from the tormentor. I guess she was referring to me". Shridhar was by now out of his initial inhibition. Doctor was lost in thoughts for a while.

"Look at this phenomenon this way, Shridhar, as I said it is usually linked with trauma due to forced sex, the victim feels victimized and becomes vulnerable or at times violent. There is a loss of contact with reality and the host person tries to create another personality that the host may want to be". This prognosis so aptly described the way Gauri's mind had worked through her life.

Shridhar looked utterly confused and at a loss for words. Doctor sensed the situation and continued.

"This dramatic disassociation causes the patient to manifest two or more distinct identities. The alter identity may differ in striking ways involving gender, age and sexual orientation etc". Doctor continued.

"The symptoms and signs of dissociative disorder, depends on type and severity. You know Shridhar, the patient can have problems with handling intense emotions and most times total disconnect with alternating personalities. Depression is another symptom".

"Doctor, this then is a very serious problem in our present society where each day a girl child is molested or rape is perpetuated on helpless women". Shridhar was perspiring now with intense emotions of being part of a guilty society.

"Yes, DID still remains a most debated, most controversial psychiatric disorder with no clear diagnosis or treatment but arises out of sexual trauma in early age".

Friends departed that day. Shridhar was a very disturbed soul having understood the magnitude of problem the human instincts levy on female gender that is spreading unabated.

Neither Durgaprasad nor any other family member approved of Gauri's nuptials with person from another religion however the opposition from family did not deter her from getting into wedlock with Naushad.

The ceremony was a happy occasion for all of the community. More for the youth and friends. They were regaling at the supposedly love jihad perpetuated by Naushad. The concept had just begun and was fast turning into a source of political contention and social concern for other communities.

Opposition to love jihad was just then gaining momentum as other communities felt that Muslim youth utilize emotional appeals and charm to entice girls into conversion by feigning love.

The beauty of Guari, enticed young and old alike as the ceremony wound up that night with friends of Naushad merrily singing,

"Allah rasool ka farmaan ishq hai"

[The command of God and Mohammed are love]

"Yaanii Hadith ishq hai, Quraan ishq hai"

[The teachings of Mohammed is love, the Quraan is love.]

This really is what happened in a small town bordering the high way between Bengaluru and Tirupati.

The disassociated identity disorder surfacing once too often.

Naushad, deserted her for other flings, after a few months of torrid physical and emotional connect, after having married with the vows administered by the moulavi. It was so easy to say 'Talak' three times.

On the hindsight though, the drift occasionally occurring with the psychological annihilation in the mind set of the woman could have had a diminishing effect in Naushad's effection.

Gauri very devastated and in poor physical state at present continues to sell flowers on the road side.

Some call her Gauri to this day and some from Naushad's place call her PAAKEEZA. The name given to her before the nikah. One can see her sleeping at night under the bus stand shelter.

Paakeeza means the pure one.

Driven to different behavior and totally innocent of whatever society may brand her as, the circumstances caused the events to shape the way they did.

For she is Paakeeza indeed.

To Cut a Story Short

Moon could be seen throwing its soft glow over the Silver oak trees standing tall as if guarding and gazing down at the berry laden coffee plants. Shekhar stared hard at the glowing ambers, shifting his attention with that known smile at Shobha, with her sparkling nose stud, shinning in the moons radiance.

Much time had flown since Shekhar had left behind his corporate stint with the MNC at Mumbai to look for life among orchards of Mango, Coconut and Holstein Friesian cows, to the anguish of Jaya.

The land itself was arid, classified in revenue records as 'dry'. The orchard was rain fed apart from a trickling borewell, leaving the plants thirsting for nourishment.

Shobha shifted the wood chips to re flame the clay stove cooking Ragi *balls for Raman, Gangaprasad and herself and looked up from behind the rising and sparkling wood fire at Shekhar. He lifted a lighted wooden sliver, to the tip of his cigarette. Refilling his whisky, Shekhar glanced towards Shobha steadily, expecting her to speak.

"Both of them should be here soon, sir" lifting 11 months Kumar to breastfeed, she opened the buttons of her soiled shirt. The child hungrily lunged towards her well-formed front

"Feed them well, Shobha, they work hard for this meal that you dish out to them every single day" Shekhar paused looking at her.

"Sir, Nagamani, that whore you employed to clean the cow shed, is eyeing my Raman,"

"I will have a word with your husband Shobha, now don't fret and make yourself miserable" consoled Shekhar,"such incidences happen and pass away without even your realizing it, keep an eye on the pot before you overcook the food, I will have a word with Raman"

"Raman will only thrash me soundly if he learns that I have complained, why don't you just get rid of that bitch, sir, and let me get on with my life, even that old rascal, father in law of mine, keeps ogling at me like an owl," moaned Shobha shifting Kumars head to let him suckle the other side, Shobha would have looked ravishingly beautiful thought Shekhar but for the soiled and shredded shirt and saree. She was wearing Raman's shirt having washed and hung for drying her only blouse.

Gangaprasad, Raman and Shobha lived on the land in a make shift rectangular thatched mud hut, tending to the plants and the four cows. Considered almost an elixir in India, milk and milking cows are revered and even prayed to as "Kamadhenu", the sacred bovine that grants all wishes.

A large percentage of this mainstay of the rural Indian economy are owned by the small and landless farmers of India, with next to nothing available to feed these malnourished animals. High cost of maintenance, low yield and almost criminal lack of government planning and foresight has forced the marginal farmers to abandon and seek livelihood as labourers.

Musing over this predicament and his own state of affairs, Shekhar glanced vacantly at the shed. He could only hear the crackling of the fire and low sound of his cows chewing the cud mainly comprising of dry paddy stalks. Shobha had already laid down her dozing child on a stained cloth, her hands busy moulding to shape the Ragi balls. These were gulped down with a chutney* or curry loaded with chili and tamarind*. She knew this fiery concoction would be what her Raman would want, after days hard work and sarai*.

"Ganga, its obnoxious the way you dig behind the rats, messing up the lands. I saw you at it again today, put a stop to your disgusting behavior or leave my place" cautioned Shekhar. Gangaprasad belonged to the community adept at roasting and eating rats, large rodents, inhabiting the farm lands. Before the old wretch could offer an apology, Shekhar turned in for the night in his dwellings in front of the fire, leaving the door open.

Gangaprasad, gulped down his last morsel glancing at a snoring Raman and addressed himself to Shobha, "you good for nothing, progeny of a prostitute, can't you make yourself available to sir? Look how he is turning in bed, least you can do is entice him to get some favours for us?" Shobha lifting her child slid besides Raman,leaving her father in law to slump next to the smoking ambers.

Permissively being at permissible level in villages.

Hot summer was giving way to greyish clouds moving with the wind, giving the impression of a flock of sheep,greyish white, grazing and moving slowly through the bluish pasture. Soon it will begin to partially wet and soften the soil to sow groundnut nurtured by the scanty rain. Everyone wanted a role in it to secure the need for cooking medium. Seed could be had from the previous year's stock, govt. outlets, borrowing at stupendous interest rates or as a simple barter between man's sweat and land.

There was feverish activity all around the village during the following weeks. Men were out ploughing the soil, constantly prodding the oxen in boney state to pull at the yoke while leaning on the triangular plough to dig it deep in the soil exposing multitudes of worms to the delight of preying crows and white cranes.

Once in a while the ox would tumble on a stone, hoof hurting but would plough on, muted, for the fear of the whip cracking on its back bringing pain right upto the aging bones. Come evening, the men would sit down encircling the fire cooking the Ragi balls* some with the sarai*, some without.

Oxen would be pegged to the stakes with dry fodder for nourishment. Gangaprasad was visiting the village to check on his locked up hut, saddened that he neither had the land nor the resources to grow groundnut like his mates, Guru and Shiva.

The sound of someone calling for him, fell on deaf ears, remorsefully he walked on, unmindful of the surroundings, the high pitched voices of the arguing women, barking of the dogs and joyful chattering of the young damsels, on the threshold of attaining their puberty.

"Are you deaf, man"?called out Shiva, voice already unsteady and tobacco smoke snarling out of the nostrils," Come here, you mother fucker,' haven't seen you in a long time." His thoughts interrupted, Ganga looked warily towards the source of irritatingly intruding voice, his lips now parting in a grin, showing his chipped yellowing teeth.

"Sit and have a mouthful" extending the bottle Guru said to the delight of Ganga who needed no prodding and gulped the contents down, extended his fingers towards Shiva's partially smoked beedi* and dragged in a lungful of the cancerous fume letting it out of his nostrils while choking on his cough.

"Take it easy man, what's bothering you?" are you not squeezing your Shekhar sir enough or is your daughter in law not giving you any quarters?" asked his friend with a hoarse laughter.

"It is Raman, I am worried about, no lands to call his own" blurted Ganga," I will see him as a labourer till I close my eyes forever" his eyes now staring at the nothingness of the pitch darkness yonder, taking another drag at the beedi * his voice fell silent.

"Use your wits, these city dwellers are suckers, play on their emotions and you will find them eating out of your hands. Don't you remember the balding high caste, chaste fellow with tuft at the back of his head and three red vermilion* lines on his forehead, who talked about some dan,dam".

Cutting Shiva's blabbering short, Guru retorted" (Sam, Dam, Dand and Bhed), you fat headed pig, meaning by any method to get your goal met". The three friends chatted for a long time and at the end of it, Ganga though in a light stupor, saw the light at the end of the tunnel. Bidding them all well, Ganga set back to the orchard contemplating.

"Sir, we have chronic shortage of water for the plants and must take advantage of the on setting monsoon, let me ask Shobha and Raman to gather as much fallen leaves, twigs,half eaten fodder and spread it around the pit of the plants, this will provide a cover over the water from rains and borewell, minimizing evaporation, retaining moisture and encouraging the growth of earthworms. Soil will become good and fertile, our plants will grow faster and healthier."

Shekhar listened to the logic of Ganga with gratitude and appreciation not knowing that the profound wisdom of Ganga percolated to him from the interaction with Non-Governmental organizations circulating in the area more with the objective of selling the plants, obtained from the Dept. of Horticulture for free distribution, for a profit, during rains, than with an eye on educating farmers on Vermiculture and water conservation.

Shekhar was unaware of section of NGO's*,engaged in such activities like distribution of condoms and preparing vermicast. The condoms could be seen selling in kiosks and the cement for vermitanks finding it's way to hardware shops. Unfortunate mushrooming of NGOs coupled with scheming chartered accountants has seen a moral decline in both Governance and commitment, ofcourse the fountainhead of the cesspool, remaining the politician and bureaucracy.

That fortnight saw hectic activity on the orchard. Shobha carrying large baskets of waste organic material on her head, while Kumar wailing and running behind his mother with a runny nose.

Still she carried on, under Ganga's watchful eyes. That's when she heard the grunt what sounded like a human in ecstasy, under the shaded Gooseberry tree, she saw Nagamani and Raman entwined like two cobras. Indian mythology has often depicted snakes as holy, also some of them as "Ichadhari"* who can assume human form at will.

"You filthy prostitute," shouted Shobha throwing down the load.

Screaming hoarsely she tugged at the hair of Nagamani whose lower garment was loosely draped around her waist. She wailed with pain and caught hold of Shobha's hair pulling with all her might. By now both the women were exchanging obscene words loudly, each holding the others hair and pulling hard.

"It is good, Shekhar sir is away, otherwise no good would have come out of this commotion, get away now. What wrong have I done when you keep away from me since the time you gave birth to your son" uttering thus Raman pulled aside Shobha' while Nagamani hurried away to the animal shed gathering around her the fallen saree*. Tears rolling down her cheek, Shobha seething with anger and agony lifted her child and went about her work giving her treacherous husband a scornful look in utter disgust.

The morning's episode had aggravated the lower abdomen pain causing Shobha to squat down pressing at her stomach. Shekhar,had shown her to the local Gynecologist who had treated her for suspected urinary tract infection and much later as the pain persisted, he again arranged for a costly scan at the city center revealing a cist as the cause for the discomfort. Shekhar had promised an operation as soon as financial issues could be addressed. She decided to speak to Shekhar sir as soon as he would come.

"I am going to press him hard to advance us the groundnut seeds, we can plough the earth in between the mango plants and sow"

"Where do you get the manure needed for the crop and also the Govt. fertilizer" asked Raman

"Use your imagination son" Ganga speaking in a low voice added," once we have mulched* the pits, the huge pile of farm yard manure from cow dung lying will come in handy, a bag or two of the govt. manure we will set aside from the twenty bags meant for plants before mulching*. You only have to see that both the women don't blurt out. Shobha with her holier than thou attitude and your fuc…. keep, out of spite. I witnessed the incident this morning."

"Shekhar sir knows enough now to demand his share of the crop, will all this labour be fruitful?" demanded Raman of his father

"You have much to learn,have you not heard of the farmer and the bear who cultivated together a rich harvest of radish? When the time came for plucking and sharing equally, the farmer offered the bear all the top green, lamenting continuously how he will make do with the portion in the mud while parting with the best. You know the pathetic supply of the fodder. Shekhar sir should be quite satisfied with the dried plants of groundnut, cows munch on them with pleasure like we do with a handful of puffed rice*."

Such was the ingenuity of Ganga, native to all deprived humans, constantly struggling to keep their head above the water.

It is a different matter that Ganga's plan never materialized, rain failed miserably that season drying up the groundnut crop. Survey was conducted and state administration distributed compensation through the department of horticulture. Neither the farmer nor the state administration was any better with the entire exercise of the season. The horticulture officer though had added two floors to his already sprawling house near the town.

Shekhar suffered a marginal loss inspite of the compensation. Gangaprasad was able to carry away what was left of the dried crop to sell the same for peanuts to the sweet shop in town making salty mixture. On the way back, sizable portion of it had gone down the throats of the three friends.

Mango plants were now in full blossom but the flowers had to be pinched off at least for five years to allow the plant growth. It is a normal practice to do so as fruits if allowed would drain away the nutrients, stunting the plant growth.

Shekhar entrusted this task to Shobha knowing her to be more careful and alert than Raman and Ganga. He did not want any plant to be neglected. Each morning she went about her task with Kumar in tow, while Shekhar followed them. This went on for two days before Shobha decided to open up to Shekhar on the subject of Raman and her painful condition.

"Sir, I cannot bear the pain for long now,' she was telling Shekhar standing next to her participating in the activity," I have pain everyday and night and sometimes very sharp, I find it difficult to eat, infact most of the time I feel as if full."

Shekhar had implicit faith in Shobha's simplicity and integrity, having trusted her time and again with cash as well as the tasks on the land or otherwise, as entrusted to her. The agent, collecting the daily yield of milk or any payment from the vegetable market yard, sporadically grown and sent for sale was handled by her in the absence of Shekhar, much to the annoyance of Gangaprasad.

"Let me get hold of some cash Shobha, I will get your operation done, just now you know how the situation stands, but be rest assured nothing will stop me from attending to your needs." Comforting her so, Shekhar walked towards the gate to receive the asst.manager of the rural bank, who he knew would have come to remind him of the impending payment of interest and crop loan taken the previous year.

Full moon often brings in gentle cool breeze giving respite from harsh summers of Indian subcontinent and times like this would bring in friends together, that is what happened that night.

"Laxman has to be roped in to part with his two acres of land to you, Ganga," Inhaling and then blowing out rings of white tobacco smoke said Guru.

"He is in debt and has no income to fend for himself and the mother less daughter of his, this will be the perfect time to make a deal with him if you can get your Shekhar sir to part with the cash needed, you can own land like us and grow sugarcane for jaggery."

Everyone knew that banks would offer crop loan anytime on sugarcane field as the end product commanded very high rate in the market, shooting up every year. It is a different matter that many would avoid repaying till the elections when the incumbent party would waive off the loans with an eye on votes.

"Yes Ganga, let us get Laxman here and talk it out with him" proposed Shiva opening the second bottle of sarai* happy also with the prospect of getting Ganga to buy more liquor for Laxman which he could partake of too

." I will go get Laxman as well as some more of this godforsaken drink to pump down his throat."

Ganga was not enthusiastic of the whole idea knowing well that Shekhar may not be in a position to finance the deal. Shiva was on his way before any further consultations, returning with a droopy eyed Laxman with his greyish stuble and unkempt hair. Squatting down Laxman took the beedi*and the half empty bottle from Guru.

It took all but four bottles of sarai* and two packs of Mohan beedi* to close the deal with Guru thrusting a hundred rupee note as token advance on Ganga's behalf. Friends parted that night patting each other's back. Ganga in a state of daze and unsure of himself, wobbled back to the orchard. That night he barely slept.

"The four steps to achievement are, to plan purposefully, prepare prayerfully, proceed positively and pursue persistently" these words by William Ward, though unknowingly were the driving force of the man.

If humans would learn from history, evolution would continue as Darwin perceived but Man's greed has not spared the inevitable. Species are fast vanishing or are endangered while genetic experiments claim to create super humans by the middle of this century. Such imbalance may well destroy the beautiful planet in time to come.

"We have negotiated with Laxman to sell his lands to us at rock bottom rates, somehow this deal has to go through, money has to be found, I want to see you owning and cultivating your own land before I join your mother peacefully in the other world" Ganga then proceeded to describe the night's endeavor to Raman, staring at him to catch the reaction.

"That is never going to happen, who will give the money and then how to get the water for irrigation "Raman questioned,

"Look here, the adjoining lands have borewells with enough water gushing off them, the stream below would yield water if tapped, let us go ahead with the land issue and think about the bore later, we must approach Shekhar sir and get the cash needed. Listen son, we must work with a plan and involve your wife into this as sir has a soft corner for her," Ganga responded.

"You have already caused enough commotion due to your recent exploits with Nagamani, now is the time for you to put on a concerted efforts to work on Shobha's diluted affection and make her a party to this. There is not much time, the deal has to be closed in three months and revenue records created in your name".

Raman did not need any more prodding as the very idea of seeing his photo affixed in the passbook given by the revenue department set him thinking of working on Shobha's mind. With his faculties working overtime, Raman devised a series of moves. An apple does not fall far from the tree.

The big Shandy* was two days away. There will be a plethora of things to buy from bangles to bicycle, if one had the money. Next day saw him making over to Nagamani's dwellings not far away from the orchard.

She was married at the tender age of thirteen and by the time she was in her thirties with two children, her husband had passed away due to liver disorder. In Raman she had seen a companion, subdued,attached, yet capable and caring to make her reach multiple orgasm, lacking pathetically in men who believed in prowess and size of their organs not realizing the importance of foreplay. Her nipples had hardened as Raman baring her had started sucking her while moving his fingers deftly on to her thighs.

"Naga, things will change' I am on to a better prospective in life," little money and your support is all I need." He entered her with the vigour that was needed to hear grunts similar to that of Maria Sharapova* at the courts during the grand slams.

Raman went back to the orchard richer by four hundred rupees that night. With a promise to Nagamani to be with her on Saturday, the day after the shandy. "There is a certain Buddhistic calm that comes from having…money in the bank" Tom Robbins said so, and a similar calm was being experienced by Raman who needed this to have all his faculties working to make things happen now.

Sitting next to Shobha, busy cooking, he lovingly put his arm around her in a reassuring manner, "I have agreed to do the brickwork in the evenings, in my spare time for someone to install the crusher, for sugar crane crushing to make jaggary. "Look, he has even given me the advance. Keep it with you. We will go to the shandy and get you new blouse and some clothes for Kumar, you have been wanting so much. It is not right that you go around having just one blouse" said Raman and started prodding the stove to remove the ash' not looking at his wife.

Shobha was not used to such gestures from him from the time her abdomen pain had started, staring suspiciously she put the plate with a large steaming ragi* ball in front of him. Next day saw them both at the shandy, while Ganga offered to keep an eye on a well fed and sleeping child. Raman splurged the entire four hundred on clothes and even bought chikki* for Kumar and a couple of maroon colored bangles for a visibly happy looking Shobha.

Raman had told Nagamani of the plans, thus she kept herself away from him at the orchard, receiving him in the evenings at her dwellings, while Shobha was fooling herself in thinking that her Raman was hard at work making the brick platform for the crusher.

Nights saw all four of them gather peacefully for the meals, occasionally in Shekhar's presence. None was wiser to the happening other than the father and the son. This went on for a while till they found Shobha trusting her errant husband and by now a doting father in law.

Almost a month had passed and Ganga was visibly worried about the deal.

"Shobha, in my life time I want to see that some lands are owned by us, ultimately for Kumar to make a decent living or he will end up being a labourer like us" Started off the bandicoot one fine evening while she was tidying up the cooking area. She nodded mutely not knowing what to say, it seemed a worthwhile idea but…

"We will have to borrow for land and borewell, work with determination and make sure that repayment is done in time" he continued not wanting to allow the process to either dilute or give rise to doubts in Shobha's mind.

It is a saying in India, that a crow among birds and a barber among men are the most cunning. Ganga would surpass the crow any time. "You could continue working here along with Raman while I cultivate the sugar cane and some vegetables to sustain till cane is good enough for crushing. I feel with the help of some village elders, we can get two to three acres, if there is a way out", Ganga was now closing in on the objective, all the while looking away from his daughter in law, but constantly fondling Kumar.

"I am sure just one or two yields will be enough to pay back the loan, also banks give a substantial crop loan to tide over till the jaggery is ready for sale to the wholesale centers. Even the middle men are always ready to advance money and pay the market price at the end and stock the product till they get a large margin from wholesalers" he continued. Shobha was aware of all this and knew that if proceeded with caution, things could really work.

"My Kumar will be a land owner unlike us," thought Shobha. She was now mentally agile and ready to engage in active participation in turning into reality what appeared a dream till now. Only she was still not sure of both her husband and father in law, however, just the thought of her son's future ignited her whole being.

"A woman is the full circle. Within her is the power to create, nurture and transform" Diane Mariechild.

Ganga patiently waited out a few days of Shobha's constant quarry about the progress and then finally after the meals that night he broached;

"Raman, I have looked at all options for raising the cash but none has worked out, it is a bad lookout for us, unless God shows some mercy and a miracle takes place."

Raman just sat still holding his head with both hands, allowing some good five minutes to pass before he spoke addressing no one

"It looks as if Shekhar sir will have to be requested" sighed deeply and contnued "only if things were better with him". Saying so, Raman lay himself down looking totally resigned and was snoring in no time. Tired as he was after a day's work and having spent most of his remaining vitality on Nagamani.

"May be I will speak to sir and see what works out, it is not myself or this good for nothing son of mine, what matters to me is Kumar's future." That nailed it, Ganga's words echoed deep in Shobha's mind and heart. Women often care more about what others think of them, this dilemma brings rise to conflict as to what they want.

"My son in law, Shankar does not care about Soumya anymore, maybe she could help in this predicament and quench Shekar's thirst during the solitary hours." Said Ganga as if loud thinking.

Shobha did not need any explanation as she knew her sister in law, a heavy bosomed woman, barely in her forties and curvaceous enough to cause disruptions in the life of any gullible.

Soumya means the tender and cultivated person in Sanskrit. Vishakanya* is more apt a name for her thought Shobha. She must act. Shekhar sir, should not be subjected to any wile designs but......

To cut a happening short, it took three sittings with Shekhar, one alone and two along with the two bandicoots, Shobha on her personal entity at stake, was able to get the land transferred in Raman's name, from Laxman.

Shekhar was stressed in arranging the finances but saw through it with the hope that the money would find its way back to him finally primarily due to the woman's character, and less due to the promisory notes, which he had made the duo sign.

Shobha had to forego her operation and continued to bear the excruciating pain, while Ganga tilled the lands availing the oxen and the plough from Shiva promising him four bottles of sarai* once the rain fed groundnut crop was harvested.

Raman kept to his routine with his concubine chipping in a bit for the odds and ends needed for the crop and to satiate the occasional demands of Kumar much to the delight of his unsuspecting wife.

Her pleadings to Ganga to give the proceeds from the bountiful harvest to Shekhar sir fell on deaf ears, who proceeded to bribe the Sarpanch* to get him a loan from the bank against the proposed sugarcane crop or using the lands as collateral. At the end of it Ganga's kitty had shrunk near to nothing as banks assistant manager was unable to convince his superior that such an advance would not finally turn out to be a non performing asset. The manager was not sure if any proceeds will be left after the boring was done. Then there was the expenditure on pump and starter. Elections too were not in near sight.

The only association Shobha had with the land was to occasionally water the Neem tree standing some fifteen feet in height with a strong trunk and flowing branches which her father in law had mercifully not chopped down.

The tree was home to many birds after sunset and also to the mud plastered little shrine erected by her for Gangamma……. The Goddess of plentiful water. Shobha, prayed,cleaned and plastered around with cow dung her little shrine twice a week, pouring two bucketful of water, thus nurturing the lone tree that had what made it robust and ever green.

"We should have heeded to what Shobha told about giving sir the money from the groundnut yield", lamented Raman, boring into his father's eyes. "perhaps he could have helped dealing with the bank manager." He continued, now shifting his gaze towards his wife, awaiting a response from either of them.

Shekhar drew a blank from the bank as his own repayment was beyond due dates and was curtly reminded of this by the manager," sorry, we are under strict instruction from the head office to avoid all suspected non-performing assets."

That night around the fire no sound was heard other than the crackling of the fire and occasional croaking from the assembly of frogs at the water tank. "Ganga, you should have told me about your having reaped some benefit from the groundnut crop as well as your having dealt through the sarpanch. I have had to cut a sorry figure at the bank," reprimanded Shekhar.

"Now I am stuck with having paid for the land with no returns coming forth possibly unless you borrow on interest from Bhai, after all so many of you are in debt of him".

Piroz Bhai was the main money lender who on behalf of wholesalers, paid advance for jaggery. Money was his, though he pretended to get it from the wholesalers as an extra leverage. This also he used as a camouflage to deduct the interest burden from the settled rate at the end. It is forbidden in Islam to collect interest.

"Salam alekum."*

"Walekumsalam."* Shekhar responded, "Sab khariyat hai, Pirozbhai?"* (is all well) he further enquired.

"Allahtala meharban hai, (Allaha is merciful) Sir"* responded Piroz I, his kurta and Pyjama*, raised over two inches above the ankles, sporting a well-trimmed beard and spreading around the fragrance of strong attar*. He had already fathered seven children from his two wives but his vitality showed no signs of diminishing at fifty plus. 'Roaming eyed Piroz' is what his friends called him when they gathered around the stall sipping Hyderabadi Chai* in the evenings.

The Muslim gentleman listened to what Shekhar had to say about the whole episode in reverence, nodding and periodically stroking his salt and peppered beard.

"I will see what I can do Shekhar Sir," responded Piroz at the conclusion of the session that night, very convincingly, very apologetically and with a very steady side glance at the deep cleavage. Shobha stole a look at Shekhar and turned away to comfort her wailing child.

Financial institutions have a set of procedures which require time before disbursement is effected. However, the money lender adopts delaying tactics to test the patience and increase the desperation in a borrower to get his pound of flesh. Nothing different happened here with Gangaprasad who after several visits to the kirana* shop of Piroz which was also his address for the lending operation, could not realize the objective.

Getting loan from money lenders is no mean task in agrarian set up. The lender tests ones patience to the very pinnacle of desperation and then there is a series of bonds to be signed with witnesses putting their signatures. Non payment results in debtor shamed publically and finally the matter going to the town court.

Suicides have been rampant by the farmers. One such case was that of Rajan who was found dead after consuming the strong pesticide just over an year ago.

He had a crop loan from the bank and then little from Piroz too.

"I will come to the orchard in a day or two," Piroz said, finally much to relief of Ganga Prasad. Shekhar's route, either way, crossed the cluster of shops including that of the money lender who had seen the slightly battered Omni* pass by that morning towards the city. That day passed by, there was no unusual activity or visitors at the orchard.

"Call your husband and father-in-law woman", called out Piroz looking intently at Shobha who had just finished freshening herself that evening after the day's work. The temperature even at dusk, was hovering around twenty four degrees.

"Both of them are out, PirozBhai, I don't expect them back for two hours from now". These innocent words from Shobha saw him squatting down as he beckoned her to come and sit as if to talk about the issue. She kept standing as the wet garment wrapped around her brought out all the curves for him to savour.

"If it is the cash you want and get your borewell done, do it, but why waste yourself on that rouge of a husband of yours, I can see to your needs. All I want is a bit of your indulgence. "

Saying so Piroz got up with the vigor of a man possessed and held the slender waist of Shobha who smiled cynically, firmly removing the hands that had gripped her and retorted "Sahib, don't you have mother or a daughter that you find me all alone and want to take advantage?" she questioned a very surprised Piroz, who was not used to being snubbed this way.

Unlike in cities, engaging in occasional sex outside of marital relation is quite prevalent in villages. Cities in India see more of rape and sexual atrocities towards women. Piroz was not seen at the orchard thereafter, nor did he entertain Gangaprasad, who however sensed the situation. Shobha never had any respite from constant curses from her husband and the father in law.

Such were the circumstances when money was arranged by Shekhar for the borewell on explicit assurances from Shobha while both the bandicoots sulked, pretending but kept pace with the happenings.

Four years had passed by since the transaction. The sugarcane yielded much money, getting used for urgent growing needs of the effluent Gangaprasad, unpaid to Shekhar.

Shobha's distress, seeing Shekhar having been reduced next to nothing gave rise to a great anguish as it happens to a woman's quest mostly suppressed, in silence under the grind of her daily life, and then when she takes off on that solitary journey, her story remains unheard.

Shobha was seen, her lifeless body dangling, that bright morning, by the neem tree...

Diamonds Are For Ever

• **Chapter 1** •

Sparkle of the Stones

Leaning against the wall of his dilapidated hut, Ranga looked at the small hole through which red ants were carrying tiny bits of food, scurrying in tidy un-interrupted line, like a huge disciplined army. Having watered his small two acre plot of sugar cane and lunching on hot rice and curry.

Ranga was just leaning, lazily against the wall.

Absent mindedly he started poking the tiny hole with the sickle he had. Ants perhaps had their colony at the spot and the soil was loose. Mud started to disintegrate as the hole became larger and the ants started to hurriedly disperse around.

He moved to the side to allow sun's ray's to fall directly on to the opening. The tiny creatures feeling the heat were quickly abandoning the hole. The passage now looked hollow and deep. Using the sickle to move away the soil, Ranga dug on further.

He could feel the sickle hit against the foundation stone. Ranga bent down to put his hand to pull away the soil. Shreds of soiled and disintegrated black cloth pulled out along, exposing a small copper pot that reflected back the sun rays.

Ranga kept staring at the object with apprehension. He had heard stories that circulate around the country side, about hidden and buried treasures guarded by scorpions and snakes. Though overcome by greed, It took some courage to take hold of the pot and pull it up.

He hurried in, locking the door behind him. Babu his son was at the nearby government school and wife Gayatri was grazing the only cow near the village side pond. The small round container sealed with a plate of similar metal gave way as Ranga pried it open with the sickle.

Two almond sized objects, radiant and glowing met his eyes. Ranga just stood mesmerized. The objects made his heart skip a few beats perhaps.

They were polished, cut to the finest shape, pure diamonds, perhaps.

Ranga, his heart beats now racing, wrapped the small pot in paper, he quickly tore from the old vernacular newspaper lying around and started to look for a hiding place for the treasure.

Un-pounded rice is stored in gunny bags in almost all households in the country side. Last harvest had yielded him thirteen bags that were stacked in two rows in one corner of the room. He chose the second bag from one row. Quickly off loading he opened the sewn up top, dug deep into the rice and carefully placed the booty.

All the while huffing with exhaustion, Ranga sewed up the gunny bag and replaced the same to its original position.

He did not eat that night.

"Are you not feeling well", enquired Gayatri touching his forehead. Ranga just nodded and continued to stare vacantly.

"Why are you leaning against the sacks and sitting, go lie down on the mat. I will make some tea for you", said the wife and vanished into the kitchen.

Both husband and wife were hard working lot with one son, studying in class sixth. The once large family of five brothers and two sisters was now fragmented after the division of land.

The small bit of land on which the hut stood was given to Gayatri by her father before his death. Documents were drawn in her favour.

"Her grandfather must have buried these while making the hut", Ranga thought to himself.

His mind was racing. The simple person in him did not know how to go about evaluating the treasure or how to dispose them.

The fire of the brilliance of the two diamonds meant little for Ranga. He was not aware that size did not matter as much did the weight. Heavier the piece more is the value.

"I want to talk to you about something but give me a promise that you will swear on Lord and stand by me in thick and thin always". Ranga pleaded, with the head master of his son's school. He was in awe of Prajapati who apart from being a capable administrator was also considered a good teacher.

"You too will gain if you will help and guide me". He added and kept his eyes fixed on the tutor.

Prajapati was perplexed.

"What is it Ranga? Tell me what is it and I will try to help you the best way I can."

The much disconcerted man narrated the whole matter to the tutor in a hushed tone.

"Just tell me how can I go about liquidating the treasure without getting into any trouble, Sir, also getting the right price is an issue".

The tutor nodded in agreement and just silently contemplated the matter in his mind before saying, "Let me see the diamonds first Ranga".

Pulling the small pack from his side pocket, Ranga took out a single beauty and placed it in his palm. The luminosity dazzled the tutor.

"What a precise facet the diamond has", said Prajapati appreciating the polished faces of the stone.

"Let me speak to Pradhan. He lives and runs a stone crushing unit near Bangalore. He has some lands and a house in my village. Let me call him up to come and see the jewels and guide us". Ranga thanked the man and went home.

Gayatri was home. One look at her husband and she knew something was weighing him down.

"What is the matter with you, either you are unwell or something else is the issue. Please do not keep me in the dark". She said, looking concerned.

"Nothing Gayatri, all is well, do not worry please". Ranga assured his wife.

That night he could barely sleep.

Pradhan was quick to respond and once he learnt from Prajapati the brilliance of the diamonds he was smart enough to drive to the place with a known gemologist.

"We shall let you know the prevailing price and conditions of sale soon, Ranga be rest assured that you will get a fair deal", said the portly gentleman trying to secure the confidence of the man while getting into the car after the gemologist had a good look at the stones.

"I shall very soon be back with the proposal Prajapati", said Pradhan shaking the tutor by his hands before departing.

"Absolutely stunning colorless and rare are these diamonds falling under grade D,E,F as determined by the Gemological Institute of America". Informed the gemologist, adding further,

"I checked with the 10X magnification and the naturally occurring internal characteristic gives the indication of flawless clarity, you are on to a good deal if you can manage it".

"Can you fix a price and customer for the same?" asked Pradhan

After some thought and a pause the gemologist said, "yes, but Mumbai or Surat is where we will have to make the deal if you can arrange the pieces to be transported.

"What is your rough estimate please so that I can make my mind up on how to deal this thing out". Pradhan interposed in all anxiety.

"Let me explain to you". Said the expert.

"4C's determine the quality of the stone, namely, cut, color, clarity and carat weight. Mother nature determines three of the 4C's. Color, clarity and carat weight but it takes the skilled hands of a master craftsman to unlock the fire, brilliance and sparkle hidden in nature's creation". He stopped for a while. Pradhan was listening with rapt attention.

"Depending on the nature and shape of the uncut rough stone, the diamond may be cut into a number of shapes like round, heart, marquise oval, pear, emerald and princess", continued the gemologist.

"The diamond cutter's skill influences the fire and sparkle of the stone. People often confuse shape with cut".

"What is the difference?" asked a very agitated Pradhan in impatience.

"I am telling you". Said the man apparently, enjoying the visible discomfort of Pradhan.

"The shape is largely a matter of personal preference and is limited only by the imagination and skill of the diamond cutter. The cut determines how well diamond makes use of available light". He stopped for a while.

"You see when cut to proper proportions, available light entering the diamond is refracted from one facet to another and then dispersed through the top or the bottom of the diamond creating a beautiful light scintillation and sparkle display".

"Carat weight and overall 4C's determine the value and these two are the finest marquise oval ones I have ever set my eyes on", said the man finally.

"So then what is your estimate please" asked an exasperated Pradhan.

"Well, you will have to give me five percent of the sale".

"Yes, of course, but tell me your estimate". Pradhan added quickly.

"I may be able to get you fifty lakhs for each."

• **Chapter 2** •

Fortune Has Wings

The gemologist was well connected with the trade and well respected too for his expertise. Finding a buyer was not difficult but the transaction would need considerable time informed the man. Pradhan knew that if diamonds were not taken away from Ranga, there was a risk involved in losing them all together. He hatched a plan.

Promising the gemologist bigger share of seven and a half percent and a request to act fast, he departed with two lakhs in cash to the village.

That afternoon after the school closed for the day, Pradhan sat across the table in the office of Prajapati. There was total silence and deep contemplation.

"You must understand Prajapati, I do not stand to gain much but god willing the deal may go through for the benefit of all concerned including you". Said the man and looked for answers from the facial expression of the tutor.

Prajapati was unmoved but asked his friend what was wanted of him.

"Look, no doubt the stones have the sparkle but the oval shape is the concern. You can talk to Ranga and offer two lakhs for the two stones." Said Pradhan adding,

"You take another two. I am getting five per piece and have to give the gemologist too". Voice was hushed and almost inaudible.

The lure of the amount was huge for the tutor, forever living in paucity of funds, as is the condition of teachers in

Indian towns and villages. What Prajapati did not fathom was the ultimate game plan of the businessman.

Pradhan, with his roots in the same village as Prajapati, in the meanwhile since his first encounter with Ranga and the stones, had collected vital information on the man and his status. He knew that a web of deceit had to be spun to get hold of the sparklers and was ready for any devious way to be able to get to it.

Meeting was arranged that evening between Ranga and Pradhan by the tutor.

"Ranga, my friend I can manage to get you one lakh per diamond and that too after a lot of efforts, you may consider this a favor done to me by him as you are a good friend of mine." Said Prajapati.

"I thought they were more valuable than that" said Ranga, disappointment showing very copiously on his face.

Pradhan displayed exasperation.

"Surely I am wasting my time Prajapati,' he said, "Here I am trying to help and all that is surfacing is lust for more money where none exists."

"Ranga, you can trust Pradhan not to take advantage of the ignorance about the valuables that you possess. I can vouch for that, rest is up to you." said Prajapati, not wanting to let go of the deal that would satiate his needs so much.

With a deep sigh Ranga got up and spoke to the duo," I will go get the stones, have you the cash ready?".

Pradhan simply pulled out the plastic packed notes and pushed them towards Prajapati. Ranga could see the cash in neat pinned bundle.

"Sir you please count the cash and I shall return shortly" said Ranga to the tutor.

As he left both sighed in relief.

"Have you got the cash for me too?" enquired the tutor.

"No, you come with me to the city and collect there, You can hold on to the diamonds till I pay you" said Pradhan to dispel any misgivings that the tutor may have. Prajapati knew too well not to contradict the business man.

All well that ends well thought Ranga, now with the two lakhs in his pocession he was on cloud nine.

Pradhan on the other hand continued in persuit of more even after making a big fortune out of the stones. His thoughts often wandered as he wondered how to get the villager to part with his house. Pradhan was sure there could be more hidden treasure buried in the foundation.

• **Chapter 3** •

Money Makes the World Go Round

'Your husband has made good money from what he found in the foundation of the house that belongs to you but has not cared to buy a wee bit of gold for you, Gayatri," prompted Prajapati.

He had been tutored by Pradhan to poison the woman's mind with the objective of getting her to sell the house.

"Look your son needs a good education to be able to get off to a good start in life and the village atmosphere or the education here will not give him the head start he needs in life." incited the man further.

Gayatri nodded in agreement. Keeping silent all the while, contemplating and weighing the consequences of the actions.

Pradhan had told his friend that he will invest upto twenty five lakhs in buying a flat in Bangalore and also invest part of it in deposit to get the woman monthly income. This in exchange of her writting of the property in his name.

"You can get a small flat to live as well some cash in bank to see you through the monthly expenses coming out of interest, while the child gets a good education," the man prodded on.

Gayatri herself having studied upto eighth standard often found Ranga to be an embarrassment at social gatherings and sometimes very uncouth. Inspite of these emotions, he was her husband and by now she was extremely confused.

Finally after some more provocations from the tutor, she spoke out her mind. "Well, I would still need a job to keep me busy and can do certainly with a little more income, say in a garment factory or something similar. You think that can be managed?"

"Certainly, I think so but I will have to have a word with the buyer and fix everything before you sign the papers, This is to ensure that your own interests are taken care of first." By now he had the confidence of the woman.

That night Gayatri kept awake pondering at the whole drama that was unfolding at her very door steps. Babu slept soundly after a day at school and game of tiring football with the village boys. He was good at studies and Gayatri knew the atmosphere and the company in their surroundings was not conducive enough to pursue serious studies.

Just then around mid night Ranga staggered in. Inebriated and staggering. Of late this was a frequent happening and now Gayatri knew the source and means from where the cash flow had come. This disturbed her thoughts as she turned towards her son and pretended to be asleep.

Ranga muttering something, slumped on the only cot in the house and was soon snoring.

It took a few days before Prajapati was able to arrange a meeting between Pradhan and Gayatri.

"I am going to my aunts house and shall be late returning," She had told a half interested Ranga. Made enough food, informed her son and departed for Bangalore after taking some money from her husband. Ranga parted with some without a word. He did not care anymore but money was slowly depleting.

The meeting with Pradhan was eventful. He showed both the woman and his friend Prajapati the studio apartment he owned and was ready to write off in her name. It hardly cost around five lakhs and was all of 450 sq ft. Not far away was the local school where he proposed to admit the boy.

Gayatri was excited though she said something about the space constraint. Pradhan shrugged saying,

"Well this size will leave you with an interest accrual of some fifteen thousand a month". Princely sum thought Prajapati and told the woman so.

All arranged and agreed upon it was now upto Gayatri to explain the advantages of this sudden move to her son. She would even promise him a new bicycle decided the woman. She knew Babu was enamored of the big Metro and the prospect of a decent schooling would entice the boy enough to make their life cherishable in better circumstances.

Only timming and Ranga were the stumbling blocks. New session at the school would start in a matter of ninety days.

Only way out was a direct confrontation, She had nothing to loose provided all loose ends were tied up.

Intent to sell within a stipulated time frame was signed by Gayatri and on his side Pradhan formulated the transfer of his tiny flat, keeping the transfer of balance money to bank and opening the account itself, towards the culmination.

"I am going to sell the hut and the land around it." Spoke Gayatri in a firm tone that morning.

The m   eaning of what she was saying took time to sink in. There was no reaction from Ranga.

"I shall be moving to Bangalore to see Babu gets better education and I a better life."

"What will he do with studies?" Ranga just brushed aside the proposition.

"All he has to do is learn the trade of forefathers and till the land."

"What can this tiny two acres yield, it has not been sufficient for any thing and we have always taking crop loans. No I am selling and moving out."

The argument went on for almost a week and no matter what Ranga tried including threats, pleading and trying to influence their only son the matter fell on deaf ears. He even sought help from Prajapati, unknowingly that the tutor himself was part of the plot.

His folly, he realized later that sharing the information on diamonds with Gayatri would have had different repercussions.

Too late, admission done and properties exchanging hands Gayatri had setted down to a comfortable life with a job with the large posse of woman engaged in packaging food for branded FMCG.

Ranga though had put up a fight for the dwellings almost in shambles but finally had to sell whatever pocession and seek refuge in the small town near the village.

What unfolded with time is a saga of stage managed deception involving greed and credulous nature of humans.

Pradhan had the place turned upside down only to find rubbles, concrete and wooden beams.

• Chapter 4 •

The Ripper

Small tea shops in tiny towns and hamlets is where the real action is, here people gather spending hours together with countless bidis or cigarettes. Usually it is here that either local politics or devious plans are hatched, usually for small monetary gains.

Ranga was a frequent visitor and having ample time on his hands, would often idle around the shop run by Ismail. Gradually the mere acquaintance turned into a sort of friendship and Ranga slowly started pouring his woes out. Ismail became more curious with time.

"Do you still have any more of those stones or you have parted with all." The tea vendor enquired.

What came over Ranga is difficult to tell but he lied,

"Yes Ismail Bhai, I did find four more of similar flare and was careful enough to hide it somewhere instead of having them on my person." He said and added hurriedly.

"I have taken a vow not to touch them till I visit the Balaji temple at Thirumala. Then I will need someone who can help me dispose the gems."

The effect of this one sentence from Ranga had an electrifying effect. Ismail had spread the word to few of his sprightly acquaintances and now they could be seen hovering around the shop. Come evening, Ranga would have his fill of liquor, courtesy the group and a sumptuous meal of curried chicken and rice. He was quick to grasp the reason for this sudden interest of people in him.

Now the need of the hour he thought was to keep the issue alive and take maximum advantage of this crave arising out of human greed.

"When will you go to the temple Ranga." asked Mohan casually that night after a few drinks.

"Let us see friend, I will check up with the priest of our village Temple and decide. Money also I have to arrange for travel and other expenses," He said meekly.

"No need to not worry about that, I will arrange. Here keep this for your daily expenses." Said Mohan and handed Ranga a couple of notes.

Now all Ranga wanted was to keep postponing his trip. Next morning he proceeded to the temple with betel nuts and leaves, some flowers and a coconut.

"Acharya*, take this for pooja* and keep this note for yourself," he said and handed the priest a crisp hundred rupee note.

"Ah Ranga, have not seen you in a long time, I have heard of your misfortune any way lord will bless you. I will perform a pooja for you," he said pocketing the note.

After some small conversation Ranga made the priest agree to tell the people he will come next with, that stars forbid, his going to perform important ritual for six weeks.

"So be it," agreed the priest and so it was. Ranga carried on receiving freebees from the people around him.

So is the greed of human race that the man was able to keep the interest of people in him growing, who all wanted a share in the proceeds. So much so that Mohan the ring leader attached a female accomplice to look after Ranga's needs.

"Is it not time you left for the temple." Mohan questioned after the lapse of six weeks. He was clearly now impatient.

"Yes, I think final nod from the village priest and I could proceed." Said Ranga, sensing the edginess. Some other excuse must be engineered, he knew.

"I will give you money to perform the special puja, Kalyanavotsavam, I am sure you will be blessed and proceed with the task, Ranga." Prodded Mohan.

"Yes that should be good, I know I can trust you with the sale of diamonds and get me a proper price, benefitting yourself too in the process."

That night Mohan was telling his accomplices that soon they may get the hands on the stones. Revelry was couple of notches more.

"Yes, You may proceed now Ranga, just remember the special day for Lord Venkateshwara is Saturday and you must perform the puja that day. I am sure your friends will help you." The priest pronounced, blessing the small group.

All arranged, Ranga, Mohan and Shiva performed the rituals at the sprawling temple. The sanctum sanctorum covered with gold plating was thronged daily by thousands of devotees. The priests were specially appointed by the board headed by an officer drawn from the government administrative services. One of the priests was a cousin of the village priest from Ranga's place and the inevitable happened.

"You must wait eighteen amavasya's before finally embarking on the task." Said the middle aged, pot bellied apostle once the kalyanvostavam was over with.

"The period till then does not auger well for you, do not take any chances." Saying so the man went about his godly work. A bundle of notes folded and tucked in the folds of the cloth wrapped around his waist. Silence followed. Ranga pretended to look crest fallen. Mohan stoically looked away in confusion and frustration.

He wanted to strangle the priest as well as Ranga. Better hold and go on with the happenings, Mohan told himself. No wonder money has a lure which has panacea effect.

Back to square one. Ranga and the female continued to live a life of ease and abundance as the group did not let off the chance they felt will make them affluent.

The wait for eighteen long months, six seasons would pass Ranga knew. At the end of the tunnel the viciousness of human deeds will engulf him.

He had not heard of the saying but was well aware that;

There is danger for him who taketh the tiger cub and danger also for him whoso snatches a delusion from one who trusted false promises.

"I have carefully hidden the diamonds well protected in the marsh land near the village temple adjoining the ancient well." Ranga told the group squatted on the wooden planks at the tea shop.

"Something or other has been has been delaying this, hope it will not be lost due to someone accidently stumbling on them or you may not remember the spot." Said Mohan.

"No such thing can happen I have the spot marked and as soon as the time is favorable I will take the stones out."

He looked around as if to watch out for some who may be eavesdropping and continued with his lies.

"I have them secured in a metal box and tightly wrapped around with the cycle tube with a metal wire all around it. This I have weighed down with a stone deep in the watery depths of the marsh."

All five of the group soaked in the information that Ranga was spewing out.

He was nevertheless pleased with the prospect of the thought having come to Mohan's mind about his not finding the right place in the marsh or the chances of someone stumbling on it.

Rendezvous continued. However Mohan took care to have one or the other from the group to be always with Ranga to keep a watch over him.

Spring followed the winter, summer followed the spring and all awaited for another three seasons to turn. Time has the tendency to fly by. Ranga had to take his chances. All this while the group kept him well fed and in good humour.

By now the man had become deft in telling lies and deceit. He constantly reminded himself and put in practice the qualities that are required to overcome any feeling of guilt that may appear to weaken his entire act.

Never let the feeling of guilt get to you, after all guilt is but a sack of bricks and all one has to do is to set it down, he reminded himself often. Review the reaction of your words and make sure it sounds realistic and very consistent. Do not waiver, Do not contradict, do not fidget but look convincing, was his core philosophy.

Most important was, Ranga had learnt to concede to smaller points, as he realized, it aids in getting off the hook on larger issues. He knew his act would not last long.

On the appointed day, he had a cleansing bath, prayed at the temple. All waited for night to fall, armed with search lights. Great was the expectation.

Standing at the edge of the marsh, Ranga addressed the group,

"I will now enter and bring out the package wrapped in cycle tube." Saying so he waded towards a shrub. Beads of perspiration visible on his forehead in spite of the cool breeze blowing. Dark was the night.

Ranga had chosen the new moon night as it has great significance in Hinduism and the moon is almost invisible being the first night of the lunar month. The choice of the night had other purpose than what he had portrayed.

In the torch light Mohan and others saw him chest deep frantically moving his hands for almost for quarter of an hour. Then with a sudden despair the man stood up with a long opened tube of the cycle with a metal length dangling through the tube.

All eyes were on the strange contraption. Unaware that Ranga had tied it around his waist hidden inside his shorts and had taken it out while he was chest deep in grimy water.

"All is lost, All is lost. Someone has taken the package away leaving this tube I had secured it with." Ranga screamed seemingly frantic and crestfallen.

So it passed, after a few days of heated arguments, occasional skirmishes the matter slowly died down.

The act of random kindness by all merciful has seen Babu the little boy go through his education with an unprecedented success.

Gayatri remained steadfast in her ways and is a supervisor at the packaging unit living a life of dignity.

The small towns with villages dotting around them abound with the stories of buried treasures, the rice pulling utensils of ancient period. Made of copper and iridium cheats further claim has high utility in nuclear reactors or astronautics.

Many have fallen victim to cheats and organized crime in these hamlets. There have been a spate of violence and arrests in such happenings.

Many a times the administration releases photographs of unidentified dead bodies, their face mutilated to the extent of non recognition.

Ranga was not seen around anywhere for some time and no one in particular ever looked for him.

Juban Pe Dard Bhari Dastan Chali Ayee

(LA MISERABLE)

Pope Francis, "Paradise is open to all God's beings including man's best friend".?

• Chapter 1 •

The Buoyant Bunch

I was hardly able to open my eyes. Even if I did, it was momentary, only to snuggle closer to the soft warmth of the source of my nourishment. The supply was abundant, sweet and just as warm as it should be but for those pests who would try to nudge me away. Blissful experience nevertheless and I would slip into deep slumber. Those pests were very rude by the way. One would come as close to me as possible, yawn and stretch his leg, most of the times poking it in my eyes. The other would often tumble over me, that fat, good for nothing jerk. Those were the days.

Only misery, I knew or was mightily scared of, was her vanishing ever so often leaving me to fend for myself and fencing against those crooks. The fat one now was upto tricks, trying to get up, moving a little and falling over me or sometimes on others with all his plumpness. The entire wake full time was indeed a big pain. I had to stand along with others to reach to the source of this nectar. Often I would tumble down.

The other thing I enjoyed most was her return after a short desertion in the dark hours, when all of us would huddle together in a cozy pile. The warmth of her body would put me in deep slumber. I did not mind the close furry contact with others too. Pain in the neck nevertheless.

Strange it felt when I felt the urge to move on those stump like body parts just the way she would. Just two steps and I would roll over. Funny the way she prodded me, nudging me to start all over again. Everyone was getting the same treatment. Funny was the day when the fat one rolled over and could not come out on his own from the small crater he had fallen into. At first she nudged him on. Lazy poke, never upto any good, could not come out.

I felt sick and was aghast when she caught him at his neck by her mouth and dropped him to safety, He had made those funny helpless scary sound repeatedly. Poor fellow, that day I felt sorry for him. I also hated those creatures who often came and carried us patting on the head, making weird noises. Fatty was the one lifted most often. Poor fellow. Strange, how I was changing. My feeling towards the bunch was softening. We would often bite, rub or goad the other with those stumps of ours.

Slowly and at times, running wobbly besides her was great fun in the ground. I loved her deeply and soon realized that she cared for all of us equally. I think from then my attitude towards all specially fatty changed. OOPS, I should not be calling him names.

Something was changing, I was seeing more things, hearing sounds and yes we were fighting in fun more too. My best mates were the small strange fellows who would flutter and rise up making funny sounds as I went chasing them. They had some long thing attached to their faces which they used to pick small insects and some things from the ground. UGH, how they used to gobble up the slimy, crawling insect, YUK. My food is YUM, and she is my sweet MUM. I would tell them ever so often. Don't think they understood.

I loved looking at those colored things, hopping from one flower to the other. Wanted so much to catch them but they moved up above noiselessly, and then would scurry about those long tailed furry ones with three lines on their backs. I would run behind, chasing but they were ever so fast and would take to the trees and squat on the branch looking down at me. Even they could not appreciate my pleading, to come and play. Those were the days,

I soon realized that we were not the only ones there. There were more like us only the looks were different. Some had a funny flat face, some were like a ball of fur. Every day strange creatures would come walking on two legs and make some noise looking at each other, pick up one of us and stare, making noises. What scared me was when they would pick one and go away in a big moving thing, leaving behind very suffocating, smelly whitish air behind. How I hated that air, it would leave me choking and with irritation in the eyes.

The two legged ones now had started giving us yum tasting things with white liquid that tasted like the MUM's food. One large plate full of the thing and we would all gather around it, pushing each other to get at the slightly warm pieces drenched in the liquid. Yummy. Some distance away, Mum would have a plateful of dry white stuff with some nice smelling pieces.

We would one after another scamper over to her trying to gobble a mouthful but would be lifted and taken away by the two legged one to our slumber nest. With yawn and a happy stomach rolling over each other soon all of us would fall into deep sleep. I am sure we looked like a dump of white, black and brown things all hustled together. Half opening my eyes, I would feel reassured as Mum came and laid down besides us.

Each day was great and I could feel myself and others growing bigger and stronger to chase those things which used to just flap and rise above. Later I learnt that the two legged one called them birds. They were beautiful people in all varied colours and made sweet short sounds. Chirp, Chirp. We were also getting more to eat and Mom had all dried up of her sweet liquid. None of us seemed to mind that as we were now getting our own plates of nice food.

Horrid was the day when the two legged ones lifted us and put us down on top of a long thing that looked like a bed. One fellow held me while the other took a liquid filled small bottle like thing with a long shiny end. He squirted some liquid out and rubbed my thigh. I was scared.

Oh! He poked me deep while I yelped with sharp pain as he pushed the liquid into me. Monster. I hated him.

This was not the only time. Again and again after few days of gap the brute would repeat the painful deed and for all of us.

Though I did not understand they would say,

"Done the fellow is injected for Para influenza." God knows why they would punish us little ones this way.

Not long then, little two legged ones came, perhaps with their Mom thing. They looked around all of us and finally the boy lifted me, showing my face to his sister and addressing his Mom said,

"Let's take him Mommy," he said and the girl too joined in.

"Ya he is so cute."

To my great horror the trio took me away from my Mom, the bunch. All the while the boy holding me in his lap. The smoky thing making whirring sound and belching fumes they took me away. My heart pounding with the fear of the unknown. My heart weeping for my lot that I was made to leave behind.

• **Chapter 2** •

My Family is Cool Dudes

It did not take me long to adjust to the new abode. I had my own bed in a large and shallow box, my own bowl to slurp up the nice warm and sweet food, my own water dish and my own name.

Rex, the lady had christened me. I was proud and only would respond to my majestic name. After all the lady told the kids, Rex means King.

All three called me Rex most affectionately but for the man who twisted my name while cuddling me. Rexy, Egzy, Boogzy he would say to my utter disgust. I did not like him.

He would also keep telling my new family of four to periodically take me out for relieving myself. The brute.

What if I wetted the house? Did he not go to that room and relieve himself inside a white bowl? Making a sort of sssssssss noice. At least close the door everyone would tell him. No he would not. Thinks he is Rex, The King, Ugh.

I was growing in size and bulk. Now one day the boy and the lady went and got a red,shiny belt with a collar and put it around my neck. At first it felt ill at ease. I later realized that it was good to guide me with on the road when those smoky killer things whizzed past with great speed.

The house had a nice backyard with three tall trees bearing large nuts. Coconuts is what they called the trees. The man called some workmen and had a tiny room with slanted roof and a gate built. This was for me. The backyard brought back the memories of my infancy and eyes were wet. However this passed and soon I started enjoying being in my den.

That morning I was lazing around in the den when a whiff of breeze blew bringing to my nostrils a smell beyond my comprehension but so nice that my native instinct immediately sensed some great thing to eat. Sudden was the rise of appetite.

The man was cooking something delicious in the kitchen and the aroma drifted through the window enticing my senses. I kept howling, moaning to get to the dish and sink my teeth into it but all he said,

"Just wait Rexy, let it cool down."

It was well over two hours of endless agony when he opened the back door to bring my dish with the divine morsels, of sheer delight and placed in front of me.

"here eat, now you will get meat every week twice." He said and stepped back to avoid getting splashed by the liquid as I urgently slurped at it in between munching on the morsels.

From that day, the man was my master and the top Cherry in the fruit Salad of my life.

The world was at my paws. I loved my family. The boy, Rohan and the girl, Shashi would come back from school and we three played. Me trying to run behind them and encompass my front paws in their legs.

Rohan even taught me to retrieve a ball.

Lady would give a refreshing bath though I if I have to tell you the truth, I abhorred it. She was kind and loving so I did not mind.

In all life, was a paradise.

• **Chapter 3** •

Unsettling Ride to the Unknown

One thing that put me off was a ride in the car. It gave me the creeps as well nausea of sorts. Sometimes they would take me for a prick or just for a drive that I sincerely hoped would never be and I wished for a peaceful stay back in my den.

That day the family packed, preparing for a long drive. I was made to settle down in the boot of the car and early morning we set out to unknown destination. I kept making the whining noise much to the annoyance of all but none shouted, just cajoled me to settle down and

Try to sleep.

It was late in the night that we finally stopped after fourteen hours of drive, somewhere desolate, unpopulated, with hundreds of trees, continuous croaking sound of something and amazing tiny lights flying around.

An old lady emerged from the house with just one big hall, kitchen and embraced Rohan and Shashi. I was led to the verandah and tied up while they all chatted feverishly. Anyway I wanted to be left alone, having fed on the way and soon was deep in slumber minus my comforting bed.

Come morning, my master, Shekhar let me loose and I ran to relieve myself. The place was huge and totally dotted with trees, plants and water, gushing through the pipe into a reservoir. I was tied up again as some people came with cans filled them with milk that was taken away. Coffee time for all and milk time for me.

This was a new experience for me, living in the country side, mostly dark skinned people doing work and many animals. I later understood about the herd of cows, that is from where my milk was got. Rest sold. Shekhar's mother stayed there with a battery of farm hands and some other people.

At first I did not relish the strange food dished out to me, made of broken rice and some blackish powder cooked together. Everyone of that area ate that staple diet of Ragi commonly known as finger millet.

Shekhar though took care to get them to cook my favorite as usual at least two times through the week.

Few days passed in fun and frolic at the farm lands in the company of my family. Night was especially good with cool breeze blowing, clear stars up above the clouds, tiny sparklers flying around and the croaking by the reservoir.

"Why don't you leave Rex with me here, he is growing into a strong Alsatian, capably of keeping intruders at bay." Suggested the old lady. My heart skipped a beat while the family contemplated in silence. The children made a wry face.

"Okay," he said, without a thought. I felt heavy in heart. We dogs have a sixth sense and we can respond better than other humans to the emotional feelings. We are more humane than the humans. It is the humans who care not for animals even if they understand.

Deep was the bond between me and the children. Next day morning while leaving, they all patted and cuddled while I kept moaning feeling the pangs of separation.

Generally, uncared and miserable life, is what I lead thereon.

• **Chapter 4** •

Act of Random Kindness

Though all faces were new to me and very indifferent I never howled or barked at people who came during the day though they all kept a distance from me for my size. Nights were different. I was let loose to roam the whole expanse of the land.

The thistles hurt me and the Parthenium grass, growing wildly, gave me an allergy that will leave me perpetually scratching. Once a robust, well groomed and clean self, now I was in pitiful stage. Just around this time Shekhar was back but alone. It had been good six months.

My heart jumped with delight at the familiar whiff of his body smell. I dashed as he got down from the van and putting both the front legs on his chest started licking his arms that were spread out holding me. He was affectionately running his fingers through my furriness.

I was not ready to leave his side nor could I stop wagging. If he ignored and started talking to others I would give a sharp bark and his palm would return to stroke my back.

Where he went I went. Good time as his acquaintances would flock in the evening. Chicken made in abundance and all the boney ones with meat still sticking to them partially would make my meal.

One day he took me to the large place where the man in a white dress poked in the painful object and shot some liquid into my body. It did pain but itching was far less later.

Why did my family leave me to suffer. I sighed. He looked at me with soft glance and caressed me as if understanding my plight.

Shekhar next morning was saying something to his mother and standing near the van and I sensed that he was leaving. I ran behind the moving thing all the way where the mud path joined the road nearly one furlong or so away. He saw me follow him and abruptly stopped and got down. Called me near and patted my back.

"Go back Rexy," he said. I did not move but just wagged my tail, trying to beseech him to take me away.

"Go back Rex," now he said slightly curtly. I looked up.

"Just get back." He said pointing to towards the lands.

I turned, looked back at him pleadingly. His finger was still pointing. Seeing no change in his stand I slowly ran towards the house stealing a glance or two at him. He was still standing till I entered the gate.

I sprawled in the verandah with my head flat on the floor and just did not look at my plate that afternoon.

Listlessly I kept looking at the winding mud road that evening hoping for what I knew was a wishful thinking. They had deserted me.

Suddenly I saw the white van winding in. I ran towards it. Shekhar halted the thing not wanting me to get crushed under the wheels as I ran along with it.

Then with time this became a regular happening. Sometimes he would come back soon or otherwise gap would be many weeks. I still would run till the road to be reprimanded and sent back.

No one can understand us. No one knows of our pain and no one sees clearly the steadfast affection we give and expect. For we are mere dogs.

Hachiko, waited every day for his master to return at the Shibuya train station. One day Mr. Parker did not return.

Hachiko waited. Mr. Parker never returned. Hachiko gave up his life waiting right there at the station without a shade and without a morsel. Japanese people have built a statue for him at the spot.

• **Chapter 5** •

Star in the Sky

Not that I was snooty but certainly being of a higher breed than others, I mean the stray ones which came in sometimes, I felt the need to distance myself.

I kept aloof in perpetual wait and every night looked forward for the friends I had made, the little things that flew around at night with sparklers on. Certainly a mirthless life without the reassuring affection of my family

The neighboring land owners and their friend who lived with them had taken charge of the brownish female of canine variety who chanced to wander around their house. The children fed her and slowly the stray one became a fixture.

The family and the children would visit the mother once in a while. They were wary of my presence. My size and the looks intimidated them. So I would be chained. The friend though was a bit obnoxious.

I think it was his grand plan which was put to action a few days later.

"Vijay, let us ask aunty and get the permission to cross our dog with that Alsatian. We will get a litter of puppies, cross bred and superior quality to sell as well keep one or two for security purpose." Prodded the friend

Vijay was not averse to suggestion of Ramesh his friend. Anyway both had very little to do than to engage in mostly subversive actions.

Vijay though was not sure of the lady's reaction.

By now I had become more and more disenchanted with the life out there. What with no medical care, no real affection and grooming.

It was not long before I was chained and taken away to be locked with the bitch with the consent of the old lady. She perhaps had no idea of the issues related to the highly unusual variation in our species, the difference in our gene like the Chihuahua to the Great Dane. I fitted in the lineage of the latter.

Generally we mated with our kind.

The room was ill lit and I was locked up with the brown one. She growled on seeing me. I tried to mollify her with a genuine feel of pity without any kind of mating desire. As it is females have to come to heat and that happens during spring and fall.

She mistook my friendly advance not being in heat as an attack and turning suddenly, howling loudly bit me on the neck. I was bleeding a little and just sort of yelped and sat in a corner. She kept barking for a full half an hour.

Both the inconsiderate humans unlocked and let me out to go away the lands on my own.

There was not much concern but for application of a liquid that gave me some burn.

I barked at each who came near and finally exhausted took my place in the usual spot.

Weeks passed. There was no appearance of Shekhar. I was itching all over specially near the neck it was unbearable. Constant scratching with my front paw was making me bleed and a yellowish fluid oozed causing the fly's to sit over the wounds.

Finally he came. I ran, stopped to scratch, ran towards him again and tried to jump and put my front legs on him as usual. The stretch gave me a sharp pain and I started to

Yelp loudly which turned into a whimper. The oozing fluid had a horrid smell.

Shekhar watched me closely and I kept looking at him for solace. He started enquiring and was clearly agitated at the happening. One thing that hurt me was he was shy of patting me or scratching my back. I tried to snuggle close to him that night under the stars.

Some thoughts, some emotions though must have flown in his conscious mind or else why would I see in him a marked change?

For one he had become melancholy, sort of in blue funk. My diet was also changed to meat every alternate day. Though frankly I was out of sorts, to fully enjoy the once, much loved chow.

Days passed, I was also taken for treatment of the oozing wounds few times but my condition looked beyond redemption. I continued to suffer. Even the Vet coming to the lands for cow's tried to administer drugs and ointment but to no relief and my condition kept deteriorating.

I remember my last journey. Short but very eventful as I was taken to the Mango orchard with the vet in tow. I kept looking back. He just stood like a figurine, eyes damp, but clearly portraying guilt and sorrow.

It was evident to me that he had decided Euthanasia will be right to rid me of the incurable and painful disease and suffering.

I just rolled over as the vet injected Potassium Chloride.

I can see my grave under the Mango tree where he comes once in a while and stands looking at the mound and at times he looks up in the dead of the night.

For I am a star.

www.ingramcontent.com/pod-product-compliance
Lightning Source LLC
Chambersburg PA
CBHW022213050726
47590CB00002B/772